I0625165

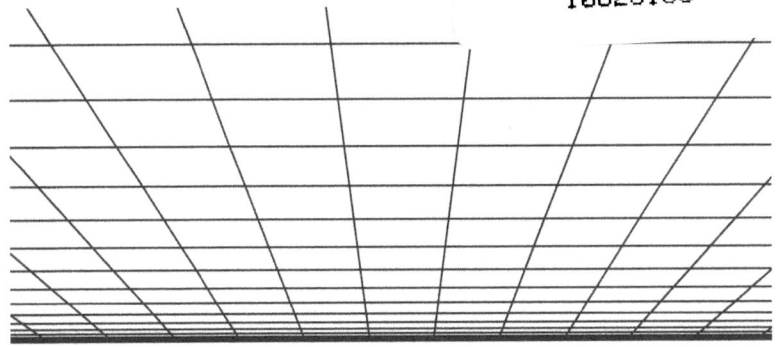

REVIVING TRISH
PROJECT DEEP
BOOK TWO

BECCA JAMESON

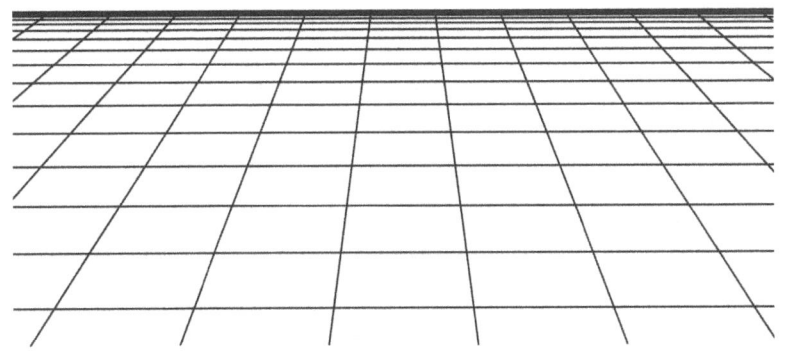

Copyright © 2018 by Becca Jameson

Cover Artist: Originalsyn

Editor: Christa Soule

All characters and events in this book are fictitious. And resemblance to actual persons living or dead is strictly coincidental.

All rights reserved.

No part of this book may be reproduced in any form or by any electronic or mechanical means, including information storage and retrieval systems, without written permission from the author, except for the use of brief quotations in a book review.

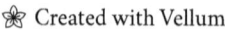 Created with Vellum

CHAPTER 1

Trish Wolbach-Anand hopped down from the rear passenger side of the truck and tugged her sweater around her body as she crossed her arms against the chilly Montana air. She inhaled deeply, lifting her gaze and forcing herself to enjoy this initial view. To the west were the most gorgeous mountains covered with snow caps.

The air was crisp and clean and fresh. The sun was shining. It hadn't snowed in a few days, so the ground was covered with gravel and white patches. It crunched beneath her feet as she stepped away from the truck.

"You okay?" her husband asked as he set a hand gently on her lower back.

She shot him a glance, reminding herself that none of this was his fault. "Fine." She hated being curt, but it was difficult to conjure up the energy for more than that one word.

Tushar might have inhaled in exasperation, but she ignored him and turned to face their hosts.

Jazmine Simone emerged from the front passenger seat, a gorgeous redhead with deep green eyes. Her husband, Davin, rounded the hood from the driver's side. He lifted his cowboy hat and resettled it. The couple owned and operated a unique underground organization called SURVIVE. The Simones, along with several other employees, were all former military who now spent their days protecting civilians from any number of threats.

Davin smiled at her, his blue eyes sparkling as he spoke. "The ranch is large enough that few people even know we have this cabin tucked away on the property. You'll be safe here. The entire ranch is surrounded by fencing that isn't easy to breach and will set off an alarm if anyone tries."

"Thank you." It wasn't her safety that had her in such a state of melancholy. It was the state of her life.

She had every faith in SURVIVE. Their referrals spoke volumes. They were an impressive group. From the moment Trish had arrived at the main house on the ranch an hour ago, she'd known this place was safe.

Jazmine hooked an arm with Trish and waved absently toward Davin. "I'll show Trish around the cabin. She's freezing out here."

Trish was relieved. Jazmine wasn't kidding. It wasn't that cold outside, but Trish had only been reanimated from a ten-year cryonic preservation three weeks ago. She was too thin and still weak. Even the mild temperatures felt colder to her.

While the two of them headed toward the cabin, Trish watched Tushar climb back into the truck with Davin.

The cabin was small, but inviting. Quaint. A porch swing swayed slightly on the front porch, the creaking welcoming. When Jazmine opened the front door and let Trish pass through first, Trish blew out a breath she hadn't realized she'd been holding. Perhaps for weeks.

She was tired. Exhausted, really. Her life felt like it was in a blender. The last place on earth she wanted to be right now was a ranch in Montana. But this cabin could possibly cure her of her angst if anything could. Time would tell.

The main room was warm. A fire was roaring in the fireplace. The attached kitchen was updated and modern. The living room sofa and armchair were a burnt orange with throw pillows in various shades of browns and reds and oranges. The floors were hardwood with rugs tossed around to add life to the cabin. There was no television.

Jazmine pointed at the only door in the room. "That's the bedroom. Bathroom is in there too. It's not much, but it's comfortable."

"It's perfect," Trish assured her, lowering herself into the armchair near the fire.

Jazmine looked hesitant as she took a seat on the sofa. "I can't imagine what you've been through. If you need anyone to talk to or anything at all, please call me. I'm not far away."

Trish swallowed back the emotion bubbling up inside. "Thank you," she managed to whisper. "I really appreciate everything you're doing for us. Don't misunderstand my mood. It's just happening too fast. I've only been awake three weeks. I didn't have enough time to spend with my son. I'm still adjusting."

Jazmine nodded. "Were you really preserved cryonically for ten years?" She waved a hand through the air. "You don't have to talk about it if you don't want to."

Trish gave her a wan smile. "It's okay. I don't mind. Yes."

"How old is your son?"

"Ryan is thirty. He was twenty when Tushar and I were preserved with the rest of our team. In fact, we owe our reanimation to him and the people he assembled to find a cure for the type of anemia we contracted and then the ability to revive us all."

"How many of you are there?"

"Twenty-two total. I'm the third to be reanimated." It felt good to talk about it with someone outside the government bunker where she'd spent the last several years of her life before preservation and remained until today.

Jazmine nodded. "That must be hard, waiting for everyone else. You must be so proud of your son, though."

"Yes. And as an added bonus, he fell in love with the first woman from my team to be revived. Emily is a gem. I feel so blessed." More emotion forced a few tears to trickle from the corners of her eyes, and Trish reached with a finger to wipe them away.

Jazmine's face was filled with sympathy and understanding. Her brow was furrowed in concern as she nodded again. "Hopefully, whoever is threatening you will be caught soon so you can continue getting reacquainted with your son."

Trish crossed her arms and rubbed her biceps. "Let's hope." No matter how beautiful the ranch was or how reasonable the decision to hide someplace, Trish couldn't shake the frustration and annoyance. Nor could she find a way to avoid blaming Tushar for their predicament.

It wasn't his fault they had been whisked away. It also wasn't his fault someone or a group of people were hunting them. Nevertheless, their relationship had been strained from the moment he informed her they were leaving Colorado. Leaving Ryan and Emily. Leaving the life she knew.

This was not where she wanted to be.

The sound of a car motor outside made Trish lift her gaze toward the front window.

"That's Davin and Tushar. They probably took a drive around the property." She stood and headed for the door.

Trish followed Jazmine out onto the porch and leaned against the railing, glancing from the truck as it parked to the view of the mountains.

"The view is amazing, isn't it?"

"Yes." Even though Trish had never met either Jazmine or Davin until today, she felt a sense of calm from this woman. And she was so grateful for their hospitality. She gripped the railing of the porch tighter to keep her balance as she glanced across the expanse of mountains. She should find the view as incredible as Jazmine was pointing out, but her mind was preoccupied.

Jazmine turned toward her, leaning a hip against the railing. "Don't worry. You'll feel like a million bucks after a few days of breathing the clean, fresh air." Eagle Rock, Montana, only had clean, fresh air. Year-round. Her smile was genuine.

Trish returned her gaze to the expanse of land in front of her as Davin, Tushar, and Davin's dog wandered closer. Davin had hair so dark it was nearly black. He was built and fit, though he had a barely noticeable limp from a war injury.

Tushar looked exactly as Trish remembered him from before their preservation. She should. For them, no time had passed. He'd been reanimated a few months before her, but not long enough for her to notice a change. Not physically at least. He was forty-five, if she subtracted the years that hadn't aged them. His dark Indian features drew her attention today just as they had the day she met him. Dark eyes and thick dark hair that complemented his dark skin and contrasted with her pale complexion and blond hair.

As she watched him move, she felt a longing she would never forget. The way he swayed his hands as he walked. The twinkle in his eyes she could see even from a distance. The lines on his cheeks when he smiled. She was still physically attracted to this man as if no time had passed.

Emotionally, she felt detached. Something was off. She couldn't decide if it had been off before they were preserved or not. He was her husband. She'd been married to him for more than half her life. And yet, she wasn't sure she knew him at all.

Tushar Anand was a good man, an excellent doctor, a loving father. Like her, he'd been a lieutenant in the army before their preservation.

He was also a stranger.

Her legs started to shake.

Jazmine reached for her arm to steady her. "Here. Sit." She helped her settle on the porch swing.

Trish wrapped her sweater around her middle as she shivered.

It was winter, but the weather had been unseasonably warm lately. Trish had always been thin, however, and nearly always felt cold. Lately, since she'd been brought back from what amounted to a ten-year hibernation, she was colder than ever. It was irrational, but it felt like the extreme temperatures of her vitrification were still hanging on to her.

"Abri is going to come over tomorrow and set up a PT schedule. You'll be back to your normal self in no time." Jazmine was so upbeat.

Trish felt guilty for her melancholy. She was always inside her head lately, making it difficult to remember social cues. She rubbed her temple with one hand and forced a smile. "I'm sorry I'm so quiet. I'm still exhausted. I can't seem to get my energy back."

Jazmine's responded kindly. "Don't worry about a thing. It's understandable. You need sleep. Some physical therapy. Good food. You'll be hiking these mountains in no time."

Hiking? Trish hadn't hiked anywhere since she was a kid. She'd had one single focus from the time she started high school—to become a research doctor. And she'd succeeded. First, she'd gone to West Point and then on to medical school where she studied endocrinology. Continuing to work for the government, she'd been sent to do classified disease research at a secret facility in Colorado known as Project DEEP—Disease & Epidemic Eradication & Prevention.

She'd met Tushar at West Point. The two had been together ever since. They had dedicated two decades of their life to their jobs when disaster struck.

The men approached the front porch of the cabin where Tushar and Trish would be staying for the foreseeable future, and Max—Davin's retired military dog—bounded onto the porch ahead of them. The German Shepard had a noticeable limp that matched his owner's. Neither Max nor his owner had escaped deployment unscathed. Neither dog nor man was letting their injuries control their lives either.

Trish threaded her fingers into Max's fur, petting him as Tushar reached her side and lowered onto the swing next to her. She met her husband's gaze. "Perimeter check?" she teased, nudging him with her shoulder. Her interactions with him were forced. Fake. She put on a front to keep everyone around from knowing how frustrated she was.

He met her gaze with what she assumed was an equally forced smile. "Hardly necessary. The Simones have it all under control. They will have someone on watch at all times."

She glanced at Davin. "Thank you. For everything."

He nodded back. "No problem at all. We'll let you get settled in. If you need anything, call." He reached out a hand and threaded his fingers with Jazmine's.

Jazmine met Trish's gaze as she descended the steps with Davin. "Nice meeting you. Don't hesitate to call."

Trish sighed as two of her protectors headed for their truck, Max bounding alongside them in his adorable lopsided way. She watched as the truck pulled down the gravel drive and then out of sight.

For several minutes she sat in silence next to Tushar as he gave the swing a gentle nudge every once in a while. Finally, he took her hand in his and squeezed. "We're going to be okay."

"Are we?" She wasn't as confident. *Okay* seemed like a distant memory. Unattainable. Foreign. She didn't even know what *okay* might feel like.

CHAPTER 2

Three short beeps pulled Tushar out of sleep, making him glance around the room. He was disoriented for a minute until he remembered where he was, and then he jerked his gaze to one side to find Trish was no longer next to him in bed.

As he sat up, she appeared in the doorway. "Sorry. I didn't realize disarming the alarm would be so loud. I woke you."

He pushed to standing, feeling much older than his forty-five years. "It's okay. What time is it?" He grabbed the gray West Point sweatshirt he'd tossed over a chair the night before and shrugged into it.

"Nine. We slept late."

He stretched his back from side to side and then his neck as he met her gaze. "Am I the only one who feels older than I should?"

She shook her head. "No. You're not alone. Besides, I'm older."

"A whopping three months." He tipped his head back and inhaled. "You made coffee."

"Yes."

He rounded the bed to reach her, pulling her into his embrace. She hated coffee, which meant she'd made it for him. "Thank you," he said as he kissed the top of her head. Making him coffee was a good sign. She had been out of reach since she'd been reanimated, emotionally at least.

No. That wasn't entirely true. She'd been distant from him for much longer than their preservation. He couldn't remember when they'd grown apart, but it hadn't been intentional. At least not on his part. It had just happened.

Now, he wanted to fix it. Whatever was broken needed to be mended. She was his wife. His everything. They had essentially died weeks apart from each other. And now they had a second chance at life.

He wasn't unaware of the tension between them. It was palpable. But he at least attempted to draw her close and start the process of getting to know her again.

Tugging her along by the hand, he made his way to the kitchen. He had no idea when he'd last held her hand. It had been a long time. Not just the ten years they'd been preserved, but before that.

When they arrived at the counter, he released her to grab a mug. "It's funny. Some things seem front and center in my mind, and other things seem like distant memories. I can picture the notes of my research as if I took them last week. On the other hand, every time I smell coffee it seems like I haven't had a cup for a decade."

He moaned around the first sip as he turned around to lean against the edge of the counter.

Trish slid onto a kitchen chair, looking unstable. It wasn't a surprise. She had only come out of her coma three weeks ago. He'd been reanimated two months before her. He considered his body to be operating at nearly 100 percent, but he remembered how he'd felt at three weeks. Disoriented. Still unsteady. Confused.

She ignored his monologue and cleared her throat. "Are you sure we've made the right decision coming here?"

He stifled the urge to groan as he dragged himself to the table and sat across from her. How many times were they going to have this discussion? "It's the perfect choice. SURVIVE can handle anything. They are well-trained. No one knows where we are. We're safe here."

Everyone at the bunker had ensured them of that. He'd heard it a dozen times. He believed it. But he knew Trish wasn't fully on board with the current plan.

She pushed from the table on wobbly legs and headed for the small window above the sink—about five feet away. The cabin was small. There would be no way to escape each other for the foreseeable future, which was probably a good thing.

He stared at her back, letting his gaze roam up and down her body. He remembered every inch of her, and he missed her. Not just from the few months he'd waited for her to be reanimated after him but from innumerable years of drifting apart before their preservation.

She was as gorgeous as she'd been the day they met. Long blond hair that bounced when she moved. Skin so pale against his that it seemed irrationally fragile. Her blue eyes had mesmerized him decades ago when they met at West Point and still did today.

He knew she thought she was too slim, but he disagreed. He still found her sexy even with her furrowed brow and the distrust written on her face. Distrust in him? The bunker? The general who ran the bunker? The government? The world? He wasn't sure. And he was afraid to ask.

After crossing her arms, she rubbed her biceps. "I spoke to Ryan this morning."

"How is he?" Tushar asked carefully. Their son was a touchy subject. He was the main reason Trish had balked at coming to Montana. She wanted to be with Ryan, reconnecting. Her mother too. Patricia Wolbach had been a steady rock in their lives both before and after they were preserved. The older woman had missed her daughter fiercely. Losing her again to a ranch in Montana so soon had to be hard. Tushar knew it was hard on

Trish also. Trish wanted to be with her son and her mother. She did not want to be in the middle of nowhere—reconnecting with her husband. That much was clear.

"Fine. He says Dade Menke is right on schedule to be brought out of his coma next week. Everything still looks good."

"And Emily?" Emily Zorich was a member of the original team. She had been preserved with the rest of them ten years ago when they all contracted a rare virus they were studying. She was the first member of the team to have been reanimated.

She was also in love with their son, Ryan. And the feeling was mutual.

Trish turned around slowly, a small smile finally lighting up her face. He loved that smile. If only she would share it more often. "It's weird to see them together. They were ten years apart in age when we were vitrified. Now they're the same age and perfect for each other."

At least something made Trish light up. Tushar struggled with it himself. "I think it's wonderful. I'm so happy for both of them."

"Ryan was always so focused and serious. It's nice to see him paying attention to something other than science and medicine." Her face fell. "Too bad we're stuck here instead of with him." She turned back around.

"I know it's hard."

"Do you?" she retorted, her back to him. She shook her head. "I don't think you can quite appreciate my position."

"I'm trying." He was. God knew he was putting every effort into understanding why she was so...angry.

"You've had almost three months with Ryan, reacquainting yourself. I've had three weeks and most of those were spent regaining enough muscle control to lift my head." Her words came louder. "He's my son."

"He's my son too." Tushar regretted the words as soon as they slid from his mouth. He cringed. She had a point. It was strange waking up a decade after being preserved to find your twenty-year-old son was now thirty, and he was in love with one of your coworkers who had not aged.

Tushar was still wrapping his head around the entire thing himself. Trish was right. She hadn't had much time. "I'm sorry." The situation was out of his control. Wasn't it?

From the moment the world found out about Emily's reanimation, people had been demonstrating at the gated entrance to the bunker in Colorado. Picketers. Religious zealots who thought the government was playing God. The media who would do anything for a story. Random protestors who objected to just about anything.

If those were the only people Tushar, Trish, and Emily had to face, he wouldn't be as concerned. But it was worse. Someone inside the bunker or with enough information up the chain of command was leaking information. Far more dangerous entities existed who wished them all harm.

This idea was cemented when Emily was kidnapped by a crazed man who thought she could bring his daughter out of preservation. There were threats. They didn't feel idle to Tushar. Nor did they feel idle to his boss, General Temple Levenson.

Maybe he was being selfish, but he had jumped at the opportunity to sequester himself and Trish someplace safe for the time being. He was doing all this for her. And she resented him for it.

She pulled her arms in closer to her body. It seemed she was always cold. Permanently cold. He wished he could go to her and wrap his arms around her and warm her up, but there was a wall between them. So far, he had only managed to hold her hand a few times, kiss her temple, touch her gently. Wrapping her in his embrace was too intimate for where their weird relationship was.

"I know." She sighed. "And I realize this adventure is not your fault. I just wish you weren't quite so...cheery about it. I'm not mentally in the same place as you."

It's like Tushar didn't know her at all. They were strangers. He realized their estrangement had started long before they were preserved. It wasn't either of their faults. It had just happened.

For years they had worked night and day to find a cure for the virus they had been researching. It had been a race against time. A race they had lost. They had been so close to finding a cure but not close enough. In the end, there had been no other options but to cryonically preserve the entire team and pray someone else completed their efforts, found a cure, and then managed to figure out how to reanimate the preserved.

Tushar hadn't expected that savior to be his own son working with a new team of scientists, but he was eternally grateful. Now, if he could just get his relationship with his wife back on track.

They had been in love once, hadn't they? Years ago. They had met in their early twenties and never looked back. Drawn together by a love of science and a desire to save the world while serving their country, it had been a no-brainer. They had become the quintessential couple. Everyone knew they would marry and change the world. But that was twenty-three years ago—or thirty-three depending on how one looked at it.

Tushar realized he needed to say something. It seemed like every time he spoke, he stuck his foot in his mouth. "We could go for a walk," he proposed.

She shook her head, still not facing him. "I'm not strong enough for that yet. Besides, Abri is coming over soon to get me started on some exercises."

Right. Physical therapy. It would be good for her. It had done wonders for Tushar when he first woke up from his own deep sleep. "Who is Abri again?"

"Abri Carnes. She's Jack's wife."

"Got it. It's going to take a while to learn all their names." Jack was one of the former military personnel who now worked for SURVIVE. Their team was going to keep Tushar and Trish safe while they figured out what to do next with their lives. "It worked out well that Abri happens to be a physical therapist."

"Yes." One word. That was all she gave him.

"I have a call scheduled with Temple later this morning. Maybe she'll have something good to tell us."

"Maybe."

"At some point we're going to have to talk to each other, Trish." He tried not to sound desperate.

"We *are* talking."

Stifling another groan, he continued, "You know what I mean. About us. About the future. About where we're going and what we want to do next." *About saving our marriage.*

She finally turned around. "You're right. But I need more time. I'm still a little angry. Don't push me."

"Why exactly are you so angry?" He shouldn't have asked. He really shouldn't have asked.

She rolled her eyes. "You pressured me into coming here, Tushar. I wasn't ready. I told you I wasn't ready. Now here we are in the middle of nowhere doing what? Waiting? There's no guarantee the threat against our lives will ever go away. Are we going to stay here forever?"

He took a deep breath. "It wasn't my idea." Not initially.

She threw her hands in the air. "Oh, come on. You practically jumped up and down when Temple suggested this little vacation. You wouldn't listen to me. I. Was. Not. Ready."

He swallowed. Maybe he should have given her more time first. He'd been so anxious to get out of that bunker that he hadn't listened to her. She was right. "I couldn't breathe, Trish. I felt like I was choking on the air in that confined space."

"We lived in that bunker for years. It never bothered you before."

He nodded, rubbing the back of his neck with one hand. "I know. You're right. Something changed. I changed. So did you. When I woke up, all I wanted to do was make sure you also survived the reanimation. Once you opened your eyes and I could inhale again, I realized the place was suffocating me."

"Why?"

He shrugged. "Probably because I feel out of sorts. After years of being one of the top medical professionals in my field, I don't even know what's happening in that lab. I feel…impotent. I needed to get out of there. I don't have the faintest idea what I want to do next, but I had to escape."

She stared at him for several seconds. "I can see that. I might have felt the same way in another few weeks, but we'll never know because you didn't give me a chance. I needed more time to reconnect with my son." She dropped her arms, turned, and walked out of the room. Seconds later she shut the door to their bedroom a little harder than necessary. And seconds after that he heard the shower running.

Shit.

CHAPTER 3

Trish stood under the hot water for longer than necessary. She had done so nearly every time she'd showered since waking up. Before the preservation she had never taken the time to enjoy a shower. She had always been in a hurry. Jumped in before the water was all the way hot, rushed through the process, and got on with her day.

Now things were different. She didn't need to be anywhere. She could slow down. She was partially forced to slow down by the mere fact that her body wasn't working at full speed yet. It was frustrating, but she was getting stronger every day.

Since both Tushar and Emily before him had made full recoveries, Trish had no reason to believe she wouldn't also. She just needed time. And apparently, she had plenty of it.

The warm water felt good. Soothing. It eased the tension in her muscles. As she ran her hands up and down her arms, she paused at her wrist and stared at the almost imperceptible scar. She'd worn an IV for weeks after leaving the animation chamber. If she didn't know better, she would believe the tiny mar on her skin was from the needle, but it was more.

A GPS tracker was imbedded in her. Ryan had explained it was meant to keep the members of the team safe in case of an abduction. She shuddered, knowing it could also be used by anyone smart enough to hack into the computer and hunt her down. If that were the case, she and Tushar couldn't run far enough to hide from any enemy.

She shook the thought from her mind. Temple knew what she was doing. As did Ryan. She had to trust the team. In fact, the device had probably saved Emily's life.

She shook the melancholy from her mind, closed her eyes, and tipped her head back to let it run down her front. Flashes of the past ran through her mind like a photo album as she stood there.

The day she met Tushar.

The night they first kissed.

The first time they had sex.

Their wedding.

Finding out she was pregnant.

Holding her son in her arms for the first time with her husband wrapped around her.

They had been in love, hadn't they? It was so hard to remember. It was so long ago. They might have simply been going through the motions. Doing what people did when they met and were compatible.

She wanted to believe it had been more. In fact, she willed it to be so. After all, how were they going to get back to where they started if that place hadn't been as glamorous as she hoped?

She licked her lips, visualizing their first kiss, the way he had stared into her eyes over coffee and bagels that morning before class. The way they had stepped into a quiet alcove to awkwardly make out so no one would see them.

They had been each other's first in so many things. Equals.

Her nipples puckered at the memories, and she ran her hands up her body to cup them and flick her fingers over the tips in order to sustain the vision. Her sex came alive at the contact, and she squeezed her legs together.

At least her female parts were coming back to life. That was a good sign. Both for her and for her marriage.

They had grown apart over the years, consumed with work and raising a son and saving the universe from horrible diseases. She knew it had been mutual. No one's fault. They both loved their work. At the end of the day they would fall into bed together, too tired to do much more than mumble a few words and fall asleep. When was the last time they'd had sex?

Trish slid one hand down her belly and reached between her legs as her sex came to life and begged for attention. Yeah, the parts were working. In fact, she planted her other hand on the shower wall and let her fingers do their magic. Hell, she couldn't remember the last time she had even masturbated, let alone had sex.

Years perhaps. Sex had slid down the priority list until she couldn't see it anymore. Lives were at stake—first the entire world's and then her own and those of her team. There hadn't been time to even contemplate sex, let alone participate in it.

Now, she had time.

She bit her lower lip as she slid her finger farther and reached into her channel. Damn. She was tight. Not just from years of vitrification, but the preceding dry spell too.

Apparently, one could reach orgasm pretty quickly after a long dry spell because in moments she curled her toes under and had to lean one hip against the shower wall to keep upright. Her legs were jelly.

To speed things up without getting caught, she pulled her finger back out of her channel and flicked her clit again. It took seconds, and then she was coming. Flying. Pulsing. Gasping.

When she finally removed her finger, setting her forehead against the shower wall, she was fighting to remain upright. Her legs threatened to give out entirely. She wasn't strong enough for this sort of thing.

A knock at the door made her jump into the stream of water

again, her face flushing as though she'd been caught doing something extremely naughty. As if a grown woman masturbating in the shower were a forbidden practice.

"Trish? You okay?"

"Yes." Her voice was wobbly. It cracked. She cleared her throat, but it was too late.

"Okay. Just checking. You've been in there a long time."

She reached up and turned off the shower. "Getting out now."

"You don't have to rush. I was just worried."

"It felt good." She cringed. "The hot water, I mean." Now she winced. Good grief.

"Yeah. I understand. I remember those first few weeks. I felt like I could stand under the water for hours. Stay in there as long as you'd like." She heard his footsteps as he walked away.

Lord. She shouldn't feel so guilty. He undoubtedly masturbated too. Probably in the shower, same as she'd done. He'd been reanimated two months before her. There was no telling what all he'd done in that time before she joined him.

The shame was they weren't connecting to each other. And now, to make matters worse, she had taken care of herself alone. It felt good. How was she ever going to find her way back to Tushar?

Abri arrived at eleven and helped Trish set up a routine to strengthen her legs and arms and every other muscle in her body. Now that she was no longer in the bunker where staff had been monitoring her several hours a day, she needed to take over her own recovery.

Tushar could help. If she asked him. She wasn't sure she wanted to ask him yet, though it would probably help bridge the gap between them.

He was on the phone with Temple most of the time Abri was

there. He tried not to bother the two of them by stepping out onto the porch. When Abri finally left, he hung up and came back inside. "How did it go?"

"Good. I just need to set my mind to it and do my exercises."

"You've never had any problems setting your mind to anything. I know you can do it."

She nodded, lowering herself onto the sofa, and leaned her head back. Under ordinary circumstances she would find this cabin to be adorable. It was small. Only two rooms—the bedroom and the living room/kitchen. It had a perfect rustic feel on the outside, but the inside was newly furnished and renovated. The appliances were less than a year old.

The perfect getaway. If a person was in the mood to get away. "What did Temple say?"

Tushar came fully into the living room and lowered into the armchair. Trish could feel his gaze on her, but she didn't lift her head to look at him. "She's...concerned."

Trish rolled her eyes under her lids, silently. Enough about their damn safety. They couldn't be any safer if they went to the moon. She was over it.

"There have been more threats."

She groaned aloud this time, rolling her head against the cushion.

"Trish—" his voice rose, "—your obstinacy about this is growing old. We're talking about your life here. Yours and mine. Why are you being so disagreeable and difficult?"

She jerked her head forward. "Because I'm hanging on by a thread. Because I woke up to everyone in my face freaking out about my safety." She leaned forward, gripping her thighs. "I woke up from what seemed like a goddamn nap to find my son ten years older and my husband a completely different man from the one I thought I knew.

"That was three weeks ago. You and everyone else have been yanking me around for twenty-one days. My brain is working at half speed. All I care about is getting reacquainted with my child and his significant other. We were in a military bunker." Her voice rose. She didn't care.

He started to speak.

She held out a hand. "It's one of the most secure places on earth. How could we possibly be safer out here in the mountains of Montana?" She rubbed a hand down her face, pushed off the sofa on shaky legs, and headed for the bedroom. She didn't want to argue about this anymore.

After shutting him out, she lay on the bed and let her tears fall. Damn all of them. She was tired. So tired. And alone.

She cried silently for several minutes, and then she fell asleep.

CHAPTER 4

After stomping around outside the cabin for over an hour, Tushar finally stepped back inside, his frustration marginally under control. The ranch where they were staying was secluded and well-protected. Obviously a fence wouldn't keep out anyone who wanted to scale it and get inside, but the various men working on the ranch were all former military and paying close attention.

The cabin was located far from the main entrance. Reaching it by foot would be treacherous. Rugged terrain would make it difficult. Any approaching vehicle would be heard from far away in the silence.

The bottom line was that Tushar felt safe here. Safe enough to walk around outside—or stomp, as the case may be. Safe enough to set the alarm at night and sleep soundly. Safe enough to keep his stubborn wife from getting killed.

He hadn't told her everything. His intention had been to spare her from the details, especially so soon after she'd been revived. He'd already been dealing with the threats for weeks.

She wasn't ready.

But it was time anyway.

He knocked on the door softly and then eased it open to find her curled on her side, facing away from him on the far end of the bed. He wasn't sure if she was sleeping, but he lowered himself onto the edge of the bed and took a few breaths. "I haven't been totally honest with you."

She stiffened visibly, telling him she was at least awake and listening.

"The threats started before you first woke up. They were serious. Many were even directed at you personally. Most were directed at me. I was scared to death."

She pulled her body in tighter, still facing the wall.

"We were the leaders of that team. Word got out and spread fast about the reanimations. I realize the bunker is safe, but the crowd outside the main gates grew by the day. At first there were a handful of people protesting and hoping for an interview. Ryan was already dealing with that before I was reanimated.

"But then the crowd grew, not only in numbers but intensity. They were no longer simply picketing or thrusting cameras in everyone's faces. They were hostile. I can't begin to imagine how Ryan felt when Emily was kidnapped." *If something like that ever happened to Trish...*

She finally rolled onto her back and turned her head toward him, saying nothing.

"It wasn't just your safety and mine we had to consider. The entire bunker is in jeopardy. Yes, it's protected. Yes, it's guarded at all times. But, Trish, the last thing I want is for a huge mob to breach the gate of that bunker and put everyone inside at risk. Not just the living, but those who are still in cryostats.

"Temple was growing increasingly more nervous by the day. She probably would have preferred moving me before you were awake, but I didn't want to leave without you. We were dealing with a ticking clock. I did the best I could to give you enough time to spend with Ryan as well as get on your feet. But Temple was growing agitated enough that I knew we needed to get out of there."

She sighed. "You kept all that from me?"

"You were fragile."

"Since when have I ever been fragile?"

He forced a half grin. "Hell, I was fragile when I first woke up. I can only compare it to how I felt. You didn't need added stress. You still don't. But I can see that moving you to this ranch has increased your stress level and I've made it worse by keeping secrets. I'm sorry."

"So what are we supposed to do? Sit here and wait for eternity?"

He sighed. "I don't know yet. But we left with a lot of fanfare on purpose, so that everyone at the gate would spread the word that the two of us were no longer inside the bunker. Hopefully it will cut down on some of the threats. After all, it's you and I they're after."

"Why?"

He hated to add this last part because he knew it might infuriate her further. "Because I made a public statement saying I was the one who instigated the entire thing. I led people to believe I personally performed the vitrification of all twenty-one people, even going so far as to imply that no one had a choice or knew what had been done to them."

She bolted to sitting. "Why the hell would you do that?"

He smiled. "To take the heat off the bunker and everyone inside. Our son. Emily. The government. The military. The country. The most important thing is to ensure the safety of those who can't speak for themselves yet. I may not have made the decision personally to preserve the team, but I did play a key role. I made an arrangement with Temple to take the heat for the team."

She nodded slowly. "I get it. If everyone believes the rest of the team had no say in their preservation, then they can't be angry with them individually."

"Yes. Unfortunately, word got out that we were married and also the last two people standing ten years ago. Your name got tied to me. And even if it hadn't, there was always the threat you could be kidnapped and held in order to get to me." He shuddered. He and Trish might be nearly strangers, but she was the mother of his child, and the last thing he would ever want would be for anything to happen to her.

"Do you think Emily's kidnapping was related in any way to the current threats?"

"No. I think her incident was isolated. That man was crazy, thinking she could somehow bring his daughter back. I don't think it's related, but it does go to prove that every one of us will have to spend the rest of our lives watching our backs."

She stared at him, most likely processing.

He inhaled slowly and continued. "There's more."

Her eye widened, but her brows drew together too.

"Someone is working that crowd. Someone has information about us, and they're selling it to anyone who's willing to pay. The man who kidnapped Emily bought her details. A reporter also bought Emily's information even before her name was public. I'm certain there are others."

"No one knows who's doing this?"

He sighed. "A man was arrested, but he was working for someone else. He doesn't know who he was working for. He was in it for the money."

"So they're at a dead end?"

"So far. Temple is working every angle she can, but it's not easy. Meanwhile, we don't know how far this goes, what the motives are, or how deep their pockets are."

"How the hell did someone get all those details?" She visibly shuddered.

For a moment, Tushar considered keeping that last piece of information to himself, but then he shook away the idea when he realized she would probably kill him in his sleep if she found out he held anything back.

It turned out his hesitation gave Trish enough time to figure it out on her own. Her eyes widened. "There's a mole?"

He nodded. "I have to assume so."

"Shit. There aren't that many people working in the bunker. Can't Temple figure out who it is?"

"There are more people there than you would think. Too many people have had access to the details of everyone working on the project. Not to mention the number of government officials outside the bunker who are informed. It could be someone we don't even know."

She slowly leaned against the pillows on her back again. Her body was shaking. "Thank you for informing me. Don't you dare keep shit from me again." She rolled onto her side to face the wall again.

His breath caught. *That went well.* "Promise." Great. This little chat was *so* helpful to his cause. Renewed frustration made him shove off the bed and leave the room. He shut the door silently behind him and headed for the kitchen area. Thank God his kind hosts had stocked the fridge with beer. He needed a few.

He also needed to figure out his next move. Obviously coming clean with her hadn't done him any good. It might have made her angrier.

He stared out the small window over the sink, sipping the beer. The cabin was going to feel awfully small very fast if they were at each other's throats. He could only do so much traipsing around outside. For one thing, it was cold. For another thing, he didn't like to leave her alone. She wasn't stable yet. Not physically or emotionally.

His stomach grumbled. It was midafternoon. Neither of them had eaten anything since breakfast. He should figure out something to eat. It would take his mind off the elephant in the room for a while.

After staring into the fridge for several moments, he decided to make spaghetti. How hard could it be?

Apparently pretty hard. He was quickly in over his head, the small kitchen covered with pots and pans and utensils and cutting boards and a ridiculous assortment of raw food.

"What are you doing?"

The voice coming from the doorway to the bedroom made him look up from the onion he was chopping. He smiled. "Cooking."

She lifted a brow. "Since when do you cook?" She looked so sweet leaning in the doorway. Young. For a moment he had a flash of her in her early twenties when they'd first moved in together and she found out he couldn't cook.

He'd felt sheepish then, and he did again now. Nostalgia made him wish he could sweep her off her feet and kiss her senseless like he would have done all those years ago. How would she react?

"Since right now." She wasn't wrong. He'd still never cooked in his life. He had a basic idea of what might go into spaghetti, but that was about it. "I've seen your mother make meat sauce and pasta. I figured it couldn't be too hard."

She leaned her hip against the doorframe and crossed her arms. "How's that working out?"

He glanced around at the partially butchered onion, the green pepper he had cut in half and then wasn't sure about the seeds, the jar of sauce he'd already poured into a pan before deciding that probably wasn't supposed to be the first step... "Not well."

She finally smiled, dropped her arms, and shuffled closer to the kitchen area. "You're going to need to throw away the outside of the onion. We don't eat the brown parts."

"Got it." He grabbed the small trash can, dragged it closer, and pushed the outer layers into the trash. "What about the center of the green pepper?"

She shook her head. "Toss that too." She glanced around. "Are we expecting company?"

He frowned. "No. Why?"

"Because if you chop up that entire onion and green pepper

and use the whole jar of sauce and two pounds of ground beef, we'll be eating spaghetti for a month."

"Well, at least we won't have to cook again for a while."

She might have smiled again, but the best part was that she joined him in the kitchen, putting a pot of water on to boil and lighting a flame under a small skillet. She poured olive oil in it next and then took the chopped vegetables from him and sautéed them in the pan. At least he thought that was the meaning of the word *sauté*.

With very few words, she pulled his meal together, tucking used dishes into the dishwasher as she went along. There wasn't enough counter space for everything.

There was an easy bag of salad in the fridge which she tossed and set on the table at the last second. And then they were eating. Two normal people having a meal. Not speaking much but sitting at the same table.

When they were finished, she helped him clean the kitchen and then lowered herself onto the sofa. Without a television, they were going to have to get creative. Especially if it snowed.

Normal people—married or otherwise—would probably spend their days in bed, taking advantage of the getaway to reconnect.

Sex.

As he lowered into the armchair across from her, he took in this small woman who was his wife. She was curled in a ball on one end of the couch, her chin resting on the arm, her feet tucked under her.

She was just as attractive as the day he met her. No one would know she was forty-six. No one would ever suspect she was really fifty-six. It was obvious the ten years in suspension truly preserved them at their previous age. It was very strange to wake up only fifteen years older than his son.

Trish was a beautiful woman. Her long, blond hair had quickly returned to its wavy bounce. Her pale skin and blue eyes would always draw the attention of anyone around. Her features were soft. Kind. Loving.

From the moment he met her in a chemistry class at West Point, he'd been mesmerized by her easy mannerisms and her classic blond looks. What she'd seen in him was a mystery, but thank God she had because he couldn't imagine his life having led a different path. Except perhaps for the ten-year vitrification part.

He was a second-generation American citizen born of Indian parents who gave him his darker skin, nearly black hair, and dark eyes. People had always done a double take when they saw the two of them together. Night and day.

Tushar's mind was on the day he first saw her when she suddenly spoke. "I can't remember when we started growing apart."

He swallowed.

She continued, lifting her gaze to his. "It wasn't intentional, I don't think. At least not on my part. It just happened. Maybe lots of married couples get too comfortable after twenty years and neglect each other."

He nodded, his throat too choked up to contribute.

"I don't know you, Tushar."

He flinched. He knew she was right, but it hurt.

"We're strangers occupying the same space."

Her words stung. "We just need to get to know each other again."

She sighed. "I don't even know who *I* am right now. I'm not sure I have the energy to figure out who *you* are too."

He froze. "What are you saying?"

"I don't know, Tushar."

"Ryan said Emily struggled with finding herself when she woke up too. She's still working toward a new identity. It takes time."

"I'm sure it does." She took a long slow breath. "It's like everything I was is gone. I can't even be the doctor I was. I don't know a thing about the latest developments. The thought of going back to school to catch up brings bile to my throat."

He totally understood what she meant about being behind on the latest advances. That was one of the hardest struggles. After being at the top of his field for two decades, he woke up to find out he was way behind, as if he had a ten-year amnesia. Unlike Trish, he had been looking into the possibility of taking classes. It sounded like fun. He loved learning. But it wasn't for everyone.

"You don't have to stay in medicine if you don't want. You get to reinvent yourself. Be anything you want to be," he offered, hoping to sound upbeat but not too cheery. She didn't look like cheery was going to work for her today. She hadn't been cheery since the moment she awoke three weeks ago.

She leaned her head back on the arm of the sofa. "I don't have the foggiest notion what that would be. I'm a medical professional. It's all I ever hoped to be. I don't want to start over, and I don't have a backup plan."

"You don't have to make any decisions today. Take some time to relax, get physically stronger. The mental side will fall into place eventually." He hoped.

"It's hard to concentrate on anything with you constantly hovering around me walking on eggshells. It's driving me crazy."

He flinched. "Are you saying you want to split up?" *Because that is not at all what I want.* Tushar wanted his wife back. He wanted to woo her like he did twenty-five years ago by his clock. He was still attracted to her. Was she no longer attracted to him?

"No. It wouldn't even be an option if I did want to. It's costing the government money to protect us. It would put an added strain on Temple if she had to provide two sets of bodyguards."

Those words stabbed him harder than any others. It sounded like she would walk right out the door in a heartbeat if it weren't for their predicament. In any case, if this was the only glue holding them together, he needed to take advantage of it and use it to get her back. To get them back on track. To put their marriage to rights. Whatever that might look like. "I'm not in favor of splitting up, Trish. I'm willing to do the work. I hope you are too."

Another deep sigh. "I don't know. I need time. I need you to let me find myself. Stop hovering. Give me space."

Space. Where the hell could he possibly go to give her space? He swallowed his fear. "Okay. I can do that. Whatever you need."

Just don't leave me.

CHAPTER 5

Three weeks later...

Trish winced as the door to the cabin slammed shut. It happened often lately, several times a day. She was still in bed, lying on her side, facing the wall. She spent a lot of time in this position, keeping Tushar at arm's length.

Most days they kept to themselves, hardly speaking. She'd asked him to give her space, and he had certainly acquiesced. A little above and beyond in her opinion. But then again, how was he supposed to know what she wanted? He wasn't a mind reader.

Rolling onto her back, she closed her eyes. She had spent most of every day in this room with the door closed, leaving the rest of the tiny cabin to Tushar. She knew when other people came and went. She could hear him speaking to Jack and Davin at some point every day.

The only person who came into her room was Abri, however, and Trish didn't really need her anymore, so she hadn't been by in several days.

Trish was getting stronger every day, except for the fact that she spent too much time lying in bed like an invalid. She did her exercises in the room and was aware of the noticeable improvement to her strength and balance. She wasn't 100 percent yet, but she was close.

If only that same improvement applied to her psychological state. If anything, she was more depressed than she had been prior to putting up a wall between herself and Tushar.

She was attracted to him. That had never changed. He was sexy and youthful. She knew he spent time hiking every day. It was starting to show in his build. He was probably more muscular now than he had been since they were at West Point.

For many years the two of them had been so devoted to their work they barely had time for the gym. She knew there was a time when she was literally aroused by watching him work in the lab. His excitement matched hers, and their shared love of medicine was sexy as hell.

But what now? She still didn't have the energy to face the future, not mentally anyway. As her physical energy picked up, her brain remained in a state of melancholy. If she didn't snap out of it, she was going to have to admit defeat soon and seek counseling. As if there were a lot of psychologists in the world equipped to handle patients who came out of a ten-year cryopreservation.

Lately she found herself recalling the early months of their relationship at West Point, the stolen touches when they passed each other in the hallway, the heated look in his eyes when he stared at her from across the room in their anatomy class, the way her body reacted to his hungry glances. She wanted to reach out to him often now, verbally and with her hands, but she was stuck. Stubborn. When he walked by her, she considered grabbing his hand. At night, she wished she had the guts to roll his direction, touch him, stroke the firmness of his pecs.

She'd dug this hole, and she couldn't get out of it.

She spoke to her mother and Ryan most days, updating them

on her progress and hearing about their lives, but she never mentioned her depression. Was it really depression, though, when she knew exactly what she should do to put an end to the madness?

Listening to Tushar thrive in the other room sometimes infuriated her. He was often on the phone with someone from the bunker. She knew he was helping them with a project from his laptop. He was also looking at online classes and spoke animatedly about the future.

He never once pressured her or confronted her. She'd asked him to leave her alone, and she'd gotten her wish. It had been time to put an end to their ridiculous standoff days ago, but she couldn't figure out how.

Thoughts and ideas about her future flitted through her mind sometimes, but she couldn't nail them down. She needed someone to bounce them off of. She needed Tushar. Her partner. Her husband. Instead, she had continued wallowing in self-pity.

As usual, she waited for Tushar to leave the cabin before she headed for the shower. She often spent way more time than necessary in the enclosed space, enjoying the warmth of the spray of water while masturbating to thoughts of what should be happening inside that cabin instead of her pity party.

Today was no different. For someone who had drawn a line between herself and her partner, she spent more time than ever before visualizing his fine body to get off.

Oddly, while she had withdrawn from her husband almost completely, in her mind they were growing closer. Every intimacy they'd ever experienced through the years played over and over in her mind in vivid color. She ran her hands down her body, gripping her breasts firmly and then pinching her nipples until her mouth fell open and she parted her legs.

In her old life, she had never masturbated in the shower. Her needs had been met first by Tushar, and then they'd taken a back seat to medicine and curing disease. In fact, she'd had more orgasms in the past few weeks than she'd had in the ten years before they'd been preserved. All while living in a self-imposed exile from the man she should be sleeping with.

Oh yeah, she was stubborn. She was embarrassed and she was stubborn. She didn't know how to bridge the gap. She was afraid of what their future together might look like. She wasn't at all sure she wanted to continue to practice medicine. How would the two of them have anything in common if she didn't jump on the same bandwagon and share his enthusiasm?

She slid one hand down her body to reach between her legs in the manner she had grown accustomed to, knowing how to get herself off most efficiently. She flicked her clit rapidly until her knees shook, and then she thrust her fingers inside her tight channel. When she could no longer breathe, and her thoughts became a jumbled mess, she ended things by splitting her two middle fingers, straddling her clit, and rubbing the sides rapidly. It took seconds. And then bliss.

While she leaned against the cool tile wall, trying to catch her breath, she pictured her husband's buff body, his dark skin, his mesmerizing eyes. The irony was that Tushar probably thought she had no sex drive, when the complete opposite was true. If anything, she had a higher sex drive now than she'd ever had in the past.

Something had to change. She needed to grow a spine.

Damn him for being so accommodating. It would be easier if he got angry and confronted her.

An hour later, Trish was sitting at the kitchen table, leaning over a book while eating a sandwich, her usual lunch routine. She held the pages down with one hand, keeping the other free to feed herself.

Abri had teased her weeks ago about her stack of paperback

books. Apparently during her ten-year sabbatical from life, the world had switched to ebooks. People carried around thousands of different titles inside their smart phones—another device she had yet to conquer. *One thing at a time.* She had way bigger issues to take care of than her technology gap.

When the door to the cabin opened and Tushar stepped inside, she wanted to lift her face, smile, greet him. Something. But she couldn't manage to do anything out of the ordinary. She kept her eyes on her book and took another bite of her sandwich.

Her husband did not behave in his usual manner, however, shocking her. Instead of passing right by her and heading for the sofa or the bedroom to avoid her, he pulled out the chair opposite hers, lowered onto it, put his elbows on the table, and leaned forward. "Enough."

She lifted her gaze, swallowing the sandpaper bite in her mouth. "Pardon?" Why did she have to sound so contrary?

He blew out a breath, leaned back, crossed his arms, narrowed his gaze, and nailed her with his deep brown sexy eyes. "I'm done with this arrangement. You've been moping around here for weeks. I know you're physically strong enough to get out now. And although it's cold outside, it's invigorating. You need to leave this cabin. Hike. Breathe. Live."

She couldn't drop her stubborn front. "Maybe I don't feel like going outside."

He rolled his eyes dramatically. "What *do* you feel like doing, Trish? Because I'm way over this routine. It's driving me crazy. You asked for time. I gave it to you. Now I'm done. If you don't feel anything for me, then say so, and we'll part ways."

She cleared her throat, but he wasn't done.

"This is insane. If you're depressed, then you need help. If you don't want to be married to me anymore, then say so. But this has to stop right now because I for one want my wife back. I don't care if she's different. I don't care if she wants to change professions. I don't even care if she has decided to become a housewife. Anything.

"I'm tired of sleeping alone in the same bed as the woman I love. I'm tired of tiptoeing around her while she mopes for eternity. We're alone in this beautiful mountain range for the first time in our lives with all the time in the world. We should be fucking instead of fighting."

She sucked in a breath at his last words. Damn, he was hot all angry and frustrated with her. She shouldn't be thinking he was hot, but it was sexy as hell.

He shoved from the table, sending the chair to the floor, set his hands on the top and leaned so close only a few inches separated their faces. "What I want to do is yank you from that chair, flatten you against the wall, and fuck the daylight out of you until you soften and rejoin life."

"Why don't you, then?" The words were out of her mouth before she could stop them, and she wasn't sorry. They were perfect. They were exactly what she should have said weeks ago.

Tushar flinched, pulling back a bit, his fingertips dragging across the table as he righted himself. "Come again?"

"Why don't you? It's the best idea I've heard since I woke up six weeks ago." She rose to her feet.

One second he was staring at her as if she'd grown a second head, and the next second he shoved the table out of the way and grabbed her by the shoulders as if it would have been far more trouble to round the table than simply remove the impediment.

The table wobbled, her glass of water crashed to the floor, shattering and making her flinch at the sound. Her book slid off the side. God knew what happened to her sandwich. She didn't care. For the first time in six weeks, passion consumed her in the presence of her husband instead of alone in the shower.

Tushar hesitated only a moment, staring into her eyes, and then he backed her up until she slammed into the wall. In less than a second, his mouth was on hers, his hands on her biceps, his torso pressing her into the wood paneling.

She was on fire. Totally alive. Restless. Needy. Greedy.

She threaded her fingers in his thick hair, luxuriating in the feel of it that she remembered as if it were only two months ago she'd last touched it. For her it was.

His hands smoothed around to grip her breasts in the same way she had done an hour ago in the shower. Hot. Insistent. Demanding. Nothing like the calm man she remembered from years ago. This Tushar was dominant. This Tushar took her breath away and left her panting.

He molded his fingers to her flesh and then pinched her nipples. Tipping his head to one side, he deepened the kiss while he grabbed her sweater and tugged it up her body. He jerked it over her head so fast their lips barely experienced the parting before his mouth slammed back down on hers and he proceeded to devour her.

She returned the gesture, her tongue reaching into his mouth to tangle with his, reminding herself of his taste and the way he stroked her tongue so sensually it drove her crazy. He'd done that the first time they kissed. She had never forgotten. Until now. But no more.

His hands covered her bra, grasping her breasts almost roughly. He dipped his fingers under the cups to flick the tips of her nipples.

She moaned into his mouth, and he pulled back. "Oh, yeah. Damn, I missed that sound." And then his lips were back on hers.

Her heart raced. She willed the rest of their clothing to disappear.

As Tushar pressed his torso against hers, his front pocket vibrated against her hip. For a moment she didn't know what caused the sensation, nor did she care, but a second later, a noise filled the room, and she realized his phone was ringing in his pocket.

He groaned as he smoothed his hand down her body and then angled his fingers into his jeans before breaking the kiss. He was breathing heavily as he lifted the cell.

Trish watched his face, seeing him fully for the first time since her reanimation. Really *seeing* him. Looking him in the eye. For a moment she held his gaze, and then he dipped his face to see the screen.

Half of her wanted to grab it from his hand and toss it away before he could look at it, but her rational self realized very few people would contact him, and all of those people were important.

"It's Ryan." He stuffed it back in his jeans. "I'll call him back."

She agreed, lifting up to kiss him again. The moment their lips touched, *her* phone started ringing.

"Shit," Tushar whispered, deflated. "Guess you better answer."

She swallowed, staring at him for a few seconds before he released her so she could pad across the room and grab her phone from the counter. Also Ryan. Something could be wrong. Something might have happened. She lifted the cell, "Hey, hon."

"Hey, Mom. How are you? I tried to call Dad. He didn't answer."

She glanced at Tushar, her face flushing. "Yeah, he's here. He just didn't get to his phone in time. I'll put you on speaker." It was difficult to control her breathing so he wouldn't hear the panting in her voice.

Tushar had righted the table and squared it back into its spot in the center of the kitchen. Half of her sandwich, her book, broken glass, and spilled water remained on the floor, a reminder that moments ago her husband had pulled out a new side of himself and made her blood pump.

After tapping the speaker symbol on the screen, she set the phone on the table, took her sweater from Tushar's outstretched hand, and tugged it over her head.

"Hi, Ryan. I'm here too," Tushar said, lowering onto a chair while reaching for Trish.

It felt far more natural to take his hand and step between his legs than to ignore him like she had for the last several weeks.

Tushar's hand settled on her lower back as they both leaned in to speak to Ryan.

Unfortunately, Ryan sighed.

"What's wrong?" Tushar asked.

"It's just chaotic here and stressful."

"Anything new?" Trish asked, her spine stiffening.

"The tension of not knowing who's leaking information about the project is putting everyone on the team on edge. Stress makes people snap. No one knows who to trust. Mistakes get made under pressure."

"Mistakes?" Tushar's brows lifted.

"Yeah. Nothing earth-shattering so far, but I don't like to see any mistakes in the lab."

"Of course." Now his brows furrowed. "I didn't like them when I was in charge either."

Ryan was the leader of the new team of twelve, the team that had come in and restarted the project several years after the original team was preserved. Ryan was the one who fought hard to go to medical school and dedicated his life to finding a cure for the specific illness the first team had all succumbed to.

Trish had always known her son to be tenacious and hardworking even when she last saw him when he was only twenty years old. He had never given up, not only in finding a cure but also organizing a team of cryonicists to ensure the team could be revived. He had done the hard work of getting the government to reopen the lab and organizing the funding to do so.

Without Ryan, Trish would not be standing in this cabin today with her husband by her side.

"What kind of mistakes are you seeing?" Trish asked.

Ryan expelled a long breath. She could picture him leaning back in his desk chair, running a hand through his hair, facing the ceiling. "Some numbers were transposed on a spreadsheet, changing the data and giving erroneous results to one of the studies we're working on."

"Transposed? Do you know who did it?" Tushar asked, grimacing. Trish knew he hated to blame any member of the team, but the truth was they would need to know and ensure it never happened again.

"Technically, yes. But I'm inclined to believe it wasn't human error. I have never once in the time I've been here known any of the lab techs to transpose numbers. I think there's something wrong with the computer software personally. But how the hell would anyone prove that?"

"Have there been any other incidents?" Trish asked. Goose bumps rose on her skin, and she rubbed her arms to chase away the chill. She'd seen errors in her life, even in that very lab, but they were few and far between.

"Not since the beaker."

"The beaker?" Trish righted herself, glancing down at Tushar. "What beaker?" The chill running down her arms changed to a frigid stiffness. A beaker incident was what started this saga. A stupid beaker that exploded in the lab eleven years ago and infected everyone in the bunker with the virus that eventually led to their cryonic preservation.

Hearing there was another beaker incident sent all the blood rushing from her face until she thought she might faint.

She could tell by the look on Tushar's face that he already knew this story. Why hadn't he said something?

"Yeah," Ryan continued. "Happened before you were reanimated. Must have been faulty glass or something. It exploded, sending shards of glass all over the lab."

Trish's mouth was so dry it became difficult to speak. "What was in it?"

41

"Luckily nothing. But it scared Emily to death. That's when I found out you had had a similar experience more than a decade ago. I think she went into shock, reliving that day. No one else in the lab on my team knew about the previous incident, so they simply cleaned it up and moved on."

"That's…crazy. How many beakers explode in the US each year?"

"Not many." Ryan gave a half-hearted chuckle. "Believe me. I googled it. Turns out no one keeps that sort of data."

Trish chewed on her bottom lip. She understood how Emily would have felt. Even the sound of broken glass would haunt Trish for the rest of her life. It had startled her minutes ago when Tushar knocked her water on the floor.

"Don't worry. I didn't call to freak you two out. I'm sorry. I'm sure it's nothing. I'm just exhausted. And now that damn data has to be redone. Puts us behind on that study. Nothing we can't handle. Not life threatening. Just annoying. I have bigger problems on my plate than that data. Trust me."

"Bigger problems? Like what?" Tushar winced.

Ryan groaned. "Did I say that out loud? Lord. I'm tired. I need sleep."

"Are you going to expand on that thought?"

"Nope. You have your own issues to deal with. Concentrate on getting Mom healthy and staying under the radar. I've got the bunker under control."

"Well, be careful." Trish set her palms on the table to steady herself and took several deep breaths. Ryan's tone indicated he was trying to sound more optimistic than he was actually feeling. Something was going on in the lab, and she wanted to be there.

"We will. Don't worry, Mom. How are you guys doing? How's the vacation in Montana?" She could hear the forced lift of his voice as he changed the subject.

Tushar cleared his throat. "It's good. Fresh air. Silence. No transposed numbers to worry about." He glanced at the floor where the shards still rested. "We did break a glass." His chuckle was as forced as Ryan's optimistic voice.

"Sounds like a good story," Ryan said.

Trish flushed, shaking her head at her husband. No way did she want him to tell their son he had shoved the table out of the way, knocking the glass to the floor so he could get his lips on hers faster than going around the table.

He grinned. "Not an interesting story. Just a dropped glass."

"Okay, well, I need to get back to work. I don't see much sleep in my future. We were behind on that study as it was. With this setback, we'll have to work double time."

"Just make sure you're all alert enough to avoid mistakes, Ryan. Sleep deprivation is the first cause of errors."

"We will. Love you guys."

"Love you too," Trish returned before the call ended. She shoved herself away from the table and out of Tushar's reach.

"You okay?" he asked, his voice tentative.

She rubbed her temples and stomped toward the living area where she started pacing away from the broken glass. "No. I don't like this situation at all." She shot him a look. "A broken beaker? Seriously? That's insane. And now this data? Not to mention whatever he *didn't* tell us."

"Yeah, I caught that too. As for the data, I wouldn't get too upset. Accidents happen. It's not an epidemic, just a few odd errors."

"Epidemic? Really? That's the word you choose to describe a study that's now behind, a study that's undoubtedly meant to prevent an actual medical epidemic?"

He winced as he stood and took a few steps toward her. "Probably not the best choice in vocabulary. No."

"We have to go back."

His shoulders dropped. "We can't go back. And we are not."

"We have to. Ryan needs us. If he had two more sets of eyes on this data, it could get reentered faster and the study would be back on track. I might not be up-to-date on the latest in medical research, but I can enter data. You can too." This was the first time she'd felt a renewed passion for her career. Maybe there was hope for her yet.

"We don't have that option, Trish. We aren't here voluntarily."

She rubbed her forehead, staring at the floor. "Then we need to undo that order. Call Temple. Tell her we're coming back. There's work to be done while the two of us vacation at a ranch in another state. It's crazy."

"Vacation?" His voice rose. "You call this a vacation?"

She shot him a glare.

His face was red, his hands fisted at his sides. "Trish, a vacation is when two people enjoy each other's company and relax while staring at the mountains and sipping wine. Except for the thirty seconds right before Ryan called, I wouldn't qualify this trip to the foothills of the mountains of Montana as a vacation." He was pissed.

She set her hands on her hips and glared back at him. "A vacation also requires both parties to agree to the trip and the destination. It doesn't usually involve being forced to leave home without any input."

Tushar leaned closer, his feet planted wide. She was surprised at his restraint. "For God's sake, Trish, let it go. We were sent here to keep us safe. Alive. It won't do a bit of good to the team if the damn bunker is breached because some asshole wants to kill us."

"That may be, but there have been no new threats since we left, and Ryan needs us." She was every bit as angry as him, her words coming out clipped.

"I can't do this right now. If you want to continue to wallow in your pity party, do it without me." He spun around and stomped toward the door, grabbing his coat off a hook. Two seconds later he was outside, the heavy wood slamming shut. She could hear his footfalls on the porch and then the stairs. And then he was gone.

Dammit.

CHAPTER 6

Tushar tugged his phone out of his pocket and called Davin.

"Hey, Tushar. Everything okay?"

"Yeah. I'm taking the four-by-four and heading toward the shooting range. Just wanted you to know. Trish is in the cabin."

"Got it. Need to blow off steam?"

"Something like that."

"Okay. I'll meet you over there. I haven't shot in a few days myself."

Fifteen minutes later, Tushar was staring down the barrel of his pistol, lining up his first shot. There were several things that had seemed like riding a bike after waking up from a ten-year hibernation. Shooting was one of them. The muscle memory was there, but the strength was not. The recoil was more forceful than he remembered.

He had come to Davin's outdoor range several times in the last few weeks to regain his bearings where weapons were concerned. It could be important one day. Even though he and Trish were no longer in the army, he reasoned they should still find a way to get their bodies back in shape and relearn any previous skills. Trish had obviously not joined him in this venture yet, but he had been hopeful.

An hour ago, he'd seen the first sane moments from her in a long while. And then poof. One phone call from Ryan and she was right back where she started. Bitter. Angry. Blaming him for the fact that they were currently sequestered in Montana for the foreseeable future.

He took aim and fired. Hitting the target—the usual black outline of a human man—right in the forehead. At least he could do one thing right.

His next shot was equally damaging to the imaginary guy. And so he continued. When he finally stepped back from the covered shooting stand after several rounds, he found Davin grinning behind him. "You feel better?"

Tushar smirked. "Maybe."

Davin nodded toward the target. "I'm pretty sure some of your shots actually went through the same hole as previous shots. We'll never even know how many times that guy died today," he joked.

"At least I didn't miss."

Davin chuckled. "Nope. Indeed, you did not."

Tushar set his gun down and then leaned against the railing of the protective stand.

"I assume your aggravation has something to do with your wife?"

"Yeah." He decided to tell Davin some of the story. Maybe the man could provide some advice. "She never wanted to come here in the first place, and she hasn't stopped reminding me for three weeks."

Davin cringed. "Damn. That's rough. And here I thought my cabin hidden at the foothills of the mountains would make any woman swoon just from the views alone."

"Apparently not Trish." *Of course, you did ambush her into coming and then kept secrets from her.*

"Anything I can do?"

Tushar shook his head. "Unless you're capable of inhabiting my body and manning up with an apology."

"Nope. I have enough trouble owning my own mistakes. Can't take on yours. Sorry." Davin stepped into the shooting stand next to Tushar and lifted his weapon. After firing five rounds, he stepped back and met Tushar's gaze. "The only advice I can offer is to say that hanging around watching me take target practice is not going to endear you to your wife."

Tushar shoved off the wall and sighed. "You're right. Thanks."

Davin didn't respond, but Tushar didn't look back either. He needed to stop hiding from Trish and confront her. He'd had the balls to do so a few hours ago, and before Ryan called, his plan seemed to have been working brilliantly. He could do it again.

Trish was pacing the small cabin when she heard the four-by-four pull up. She hadn't expected him to return so soon, and she wasn't sure it was even a good thing since she was still nursing a serious mad.

However, they needed to work this out. Talk. Clear the air. Find some way to be civil with each other. She forced herself to lower her crossed arms so she wouldn't appear antagonistic as he opened the front door.

His shoulders were low. He looked defeated. He locked the door and dropped the key to the four-by-four on the counter. When he faced her, they remained silent, assessing each other.

"I shouldn't have walked out," he stated, surprising her.

She nodded as a chill crawled up her body. "I'd rather you didn't leave me here alone like that. It unnerves me, especially since according to you I'm in serious danger. You left me with no transportation. I'm not even sure if there's a weapon in this cabin."

It was absurd they hadn't discussed how she would protect herself.

"You're right. Not to make excuses, but someone was watching the cabin the entire time. Someone always is."

She swallowed. That was good to know.

"There's a Glock tucked between the mattress on both sides. They're loaded."

She gave another sharp nod. Also important to know.

He came farther into the room and flopped down on the couch, running a hand through his thick hair. "I went to the shooting range."

"Feel better?" she asked, remembering how he would do that in the past to blow off steam. It made him an excellent marksman a decade ago.

He smiled. "Yeah. And also worse. I need you to understand that the reason we're here is for your safety. I spoke to Temple about this plan at length many times. I took a risk when I put myself out there and told the media the entire project rested on my shoulders. I did that to protect the rest of the team, for all the good it might have done."

"I understand, but you did that without consulting me."

He nodded. "I did. And it probably wasn't my best-laid plan. The decision was quickly formulated and used as a stopgap to get the mass of people surrounding the front gate of the bunker to calm down. If they channeled their anger toward one person, perhaps they would stop attacking everyone else who is revived. Including you."

"Except I'm your wife."

"Right. Minor detail."

A thought went through her mind that disturbed her. "Were you hoping you could leave without me and go on with your life?"

He jerked, his eyes widening. "No. Never. God, Trish. No. From the moment I woke up, the only thing on my mind was getting you back and making sure you were safe."

"Ensuring my safety has nothing to do with how you feel about me. I would put my life on the line for every member of our team if it meant they each had a fighting chance to live. We're doctors. We do that. I know you would too. That doesn't mean I want to spend the rest of my life with any one of them. It's just human decency."

He stared at her, several heartbeats going by before he spoke. "Don't do that."

"Do what?" If he shut down now and wouldn't discuss this with her, they were doomed.

"Don't act like I don't have feelings for you. It's not true. I realize we were spending less time together in the last year before we were preserved, but I never stopped loving you. We were dedicated to saving lives. It was important. Time was of the essence. By your logic I could accuse you of the same thing."

He was right. But she'd needed to hear him say those words. *I never stopped loving you.* She also needed him to stop tiptoeing around her with his secrets and his motives and show more of that passion he'd exuded earlier before Ryan called.

He sighed. "I made a mistake. I was stressed and worried, and I yanked you out of that bunker too soon. I'm sorry."

She pursed her lips, trying not to cry. "Could we maybe go back a few hours to the part where you tipped the table over to get to me? Maybe we won't answer any phones this time?" She fisted her hands where they were tucked under her breasts, nervous from putting herself out there like that.

Tushar glanced at the kitchen table. "You want me to knock it over again? It wouldn't be as dramatic without the broken glass." His eyes danced.

She shrugged. "I could throw something if you want." She inched backward until her back flattened against the wall in the very spot they had started making out earlier.

He jumped to his feet, stepped on the center of the coffee table, and used it to leap forward, putting himself in front of her in seconds.

She giggled at the exaggerated drama, relieved he seemed eager to take her up on her suggestion.

His hands landed on either side of her head, pinning her to the wall as his eyes searched hers.

Trish slowly released her folded arms and set her palms on his hips. "I think you were in the middle of kissing me, but you were a little closer than this." *Please God, tempt him to come at me with that passion again.*

His grin spread, and he cocked his head to one side as he leaned closer, pressing his body against hers. "You want to narrate the rest or let me drive you crazy my own way?" He lifted one brow.

She flushed, her lips parting.

"I thought so." And then his mouth was on hers, angled to one side, his tongue delving in to taste. His kiss was urgent. Hard. Demanding. Fantastic.

She melted into him, her fingers gripping his hips and then sliding around to dip into the pockets of his jeans. She squeezed his fine ass and drew him closer.

One of his hands came down to cup her jaw, holding her chin where he wanted. His other hand smoothed over her shoulder toward her chest.

She came up on her toes when he molded his fingers to her breast and gave a squeeze.

"I've missed you," he murmured against her lips without parting from her. He was still kissing her as he grabbed the hem of her sweater and yanked it over her head. He was still kissing her when his hands came to her breasts and cupped them both reverently before popping the clasp of her bra and then thumbing her nipples.

He finally broke free of her lips but only to dip his head and take one nipple into his mouth, sucking hard enough to send a jolt to her body. Her sex came alive instantly, needing contact. She wanted more. She wanted fast and hard. She didn't have a vivid memory of the last time they'd had sex, even without the extra decade, but she intended to remember today for the rest of her life.

He shoved back farther to tug his shirt over his head too, and then he reached for the button of his jeans. "Jeans off. Now."

Her hands were shaking as she fumbled with the button and then the zipper. She held his intense gaze the entire time, soaking in this moment.

Her sex was so wet he could have slid into her without any preparation. But that wasn't his style. "Panties too, baby. Now." His command sent a shiver down her body. That and the endearment he hadn't used a single time since she'd regained consciousness.

In seconds they were both naked. He scanned up and down her body appreciatively, a smile on his lips, and then he lurched forward and continued to press her against the wall.

The breath whooshed from her lungs as he inserted his knee between her legs, cupped one breast with his hand, and grabbed her ass with his other hand. He hitched her leg up, leaving her balancing on one foot, but it didn't matter because he had her.

His mouth was on her neck now, kissing, frantic, trailing up to her ear. "My God, you're hot. I've missed you so much." His tongue teased her lobe, making her shudder.

She gripped his back, digging her fingers into his muscles. She would have spoken if she could, but her mouth hung open, not a single word available for speech. Every cell in her body was alive like she had leaped from a coma to fully in the world in seconds. In a way, she had.

Tushar slid his knee up higher, forcing her legs wider until his thigh pressed against her sex. "You're so wet," he muttered. "You needed this."

"Yes."

"How long, baby? How long have you been waiting for me?" He pinched her nipple and twisted it as he spoke.

"Weeks."

His teeth sunk into her earlobe, making her moan. The hand on her ass reached between her legs from behind and found her tight channel. He had to lower his thigh to wiggle into the space, and then he thrust his finger into her.

She cried out, gripping his shoulder blades. "Yes. Oh, God, Tushar. Yes."

"Mmm. So needy. All this pent-up frustration."

"Yes." Her voice was breathy now. Could he stop talking and fuck her already?

His lips were on her neck again as he found her clit and thrummed it rapidly.

She gasped. "Please." She'd never wanted anything so badly in her life. She needed him inside her as if her life depended on it. It would be tight. He was just as thick as he'd always been, while she knew her channel was not as wide.

Suddenly, his hands were on her hips, lifting her. "Legs around my waist, baby."

She hugged his hips with her thighs.

He lined his length up with her sex, met her gaze, held it, and then kept holding it while he thrust into her without pause.

She gasped. It was tight. The stretch far more than familiar. It took a second for her to catch her breath and find her vision. When she was finally able to meet his gaze again, she found him watching her intently.

He had threaded one hand in her hair and was holding her head, his thumb stroking her cheek. "You okay?" If she wasn't mistaken, he was gritting his teeth.

She leaned forward and set her lips on his. "Move."

He wasted not a second regaining control of their kissing while gripping her hips and doing exactly what she craved— fucking her. Hard. Fast. Fantastic.

She couldn't think, and she doubted she returned the kiss. It didn't matter. All her concentration was on how good it felt to have him inside her, his entire body pressing her into the wall, his hands on her seemingly everywhere at once, his lips. Damn his lips. Soft. Demanding. So good.

And then she was coming, her channel gripping him tight as she milked his length with more force than she would have thought possible. There were sounds in the room. She was fairly certain they were coming from her, but they were unintelligible. Groans.

She held on to his back with her fingertips as if she might fall through a hole in the earth if she let go.

He kept thrusting, releasing her lips, and tipping his head back until he finally held himself steady, deep inside her, and growled, a primal sound that filled the room as his orgasm filled her body.

She watched his face, wondering how the hell she had ever gotten so far off course. This man was her husband. She had loved him once. She could love him again. Especially if they started doing this with frequency.

When he lowered his face and met her gaze, his brows drew together. "What?" he asked.

She realized she was smiling. "I've missed you."

His confusion turned into a smile. "Damn, how I have missed you too." Without pulling out of her, he wrapped his arms around her body and backed away from the wall.

She gripped him with her ankles at the small of his back as he carried her through the doorway and then unceremoniously deposited them both on the bed. "Impressive," she stated about his ability to stay inside her.

She was on her back, his heavy body a welcome pressure over her smaller frame. He stroked her hair from her forehead. "Baby, you're so tight, I'm not sure I'll even be able to pull out at all. It wasn't difficult to maintain the connection. Besides, I like how it feels."

"How does it feel?" she asked softly.

"Right. Home. Perfect."

She smiled, her face flushing. "Stay there then." She pulled him down for a kiss, wanting to feel his lips on hers again, taste him, tease him with her tongue.

They started out gently exploring each other's mouths as if they'd only met today and this was their first kiss. But the tangle of lips and tongues soon grew more intense until Trish found herself gripping Tushar's back again. She held him close, afraid he might pull away if she didn't.

She didn't want this to end. Ever if she could help it.

In minutes, she was squirming against his hips, her clit seeking friction, his length fully erect inside her again. They weren't young anymore. Technically they were almost sixty, but their bodies were behaving as though they were truly in their mid-forties after a long drought.

Tushar slid one hand down her body as he began to ease in and out of her again. He found her clit and gently stroked the swollen tip. "You're not sore?" he whispered against her mouth.

"No." She bucked her hips up into his touch to emphasize how much she was enjoying herself.

For a long time, he slowly eased in and out of her while he teased her clit without enough pressure to get her off. And then he released her clit, tucked his hands under her thighs, and hitched her legs up high and wide.

She palmed the sheets at her sides to keep from ramming across the bed as he thrust harder.

He held her gaze, his lips parted, his eyes glassy. Fucking her once hadn't been enough for either of them because Tushar fucked her again now. It took longer this time, but it felt even better. The friction was fantastic. The connection between them was even better.

CHAPTER 7

Trish awoke slowly, aware of two things—she was too warm, and Tushar's arm wrapped around her body was the cause. She sighed. Where had she been? Why the hell had she put them both through weeks of silent treatment?

The room was bathed in the first rays of sunshine. They had fallen asleep curled into each other after the best sex of her life.

Her stomach grumbled as Tushar kissed her ear. "We didn't eat dinner," he whispered.

"I didn't even notice," she pointed out, shivering at the touch of his lips on her skin.

"I need to feed you."

She turned toward him to more fully see his face. "I'd rather you didn't. After watching you make spaghetti the other day, I'd be worried about eggshells and burnt bacon. How about I feed *you* instead?"

He chuckled. "Deal."

She wiggled out of his arms. "I need a shower."

"I could join you," he said, grabbing her hand to keep her from slipping away.

"We would both die of starvation if we did that. I'm hungry.

Save the shower antics for another time." She gave her hand a tug and headed for the bathroom, feeling his gaze on her naked body.

She smiled through the entire process. Finally, a breakthrough between them. They still had issues to resolve, but at least they were speaking and not at each other's throats.

After a quick shower, she dressed in jeans and a long-sleeved West Point T-shirt and headed for the kitchen while Tushar slipped into the shower.

She had a big breakfast going when he joined her. "Oh, so you don't put the entire egg in the pan," he joked as he leaned over her shoulder.

"Only if you want them to be hard boiled, but that would require boiling water." She kissed his cheek and returned to stirring the scrambled eggs.

They were quiet while they ate, and she realized they had many things to discuss. The air was thick with this knowledge, but neither of them mentioned their disagreements until the plates were cleared and they were seated on the couch.

Tushar took her hand. "Talk to me."

She met his gaze. "I'm worried we aren't going to agree on the basic parts of our lives right now."

"I'll try to be more open-minded."

"Okay, but the fundamental problem we have is location. I want to go back."

"I know you do, and I can understand your reasoning."

"Why do you and Temple think the bunker would be in such danger simply by having us present? It's well-guarded. More security could be added. How is it more efficient to divide us up and scatter us around the country with even more protection than we would have at the bunker? It's a huge waste of resources."

He sighed. "For one thing it lowers the threat to the entire team, both the new team and the old team. There's a reasonable fear that if the mob of people outside the gates gets large enough or angry enough, they could overpower the security guards protecting the bunker. That would put everyone inside at risk. At least with us two states away, we're taking the heat off the others and dividing the potential enemy."

She rolled her eyes. "The enemy is relatively imaginary, right? I mean, all of this is based on the supposition that one or more of the people protesting outside the bunker are interested in a physical altercation."

"It's more than a hunch, Trish. Emily was kidnapped by a madman."

"But that guy is in custody."

"We don't know how many others are like him."

"We also don't know that I won't slip and fall in the shower and die from a skull fracture."

Tushar inhaled slowly. "Next time you take a shower, I'll join you. It's not very large. You stand very little chance of falling if I'm there to grab you on the way down." He smiled.

She rolled her eyes, though the visual of him pressing her wet naked body against the cool tile of the shower made her wish they were doing something far more constructive like that than hashing out their differences on the couch.

"Look, at least set up a timeframe. I'm not staying here much longer. I want to be with Ryan, and he could use my help. I might be a decade behind on medical research, but I can run data and double-check people's work. Sounds like the entire team is on edge. They need a mediator to keep them from lashing out at each other."

"What if one of them is the mole, Trish?"

She nodded slowly. "I've thought about that, but it doesn't add up. Who would dedicate their life to researching and developing cures for the world's diseases if what they really wanted to do was sabotage every project? It doesn't make sense. Both our team and the one working for Ryan are made up of the most intelligent people on earth who spent years of their lives working night and day to get their degrees. It's unfathomable that one of them was groomed from a young age and planted in that bunker to cause harm."

He sighed, leaned back against the sofa. "You're right."

"Maybe there is no mole. Maybe we're overreacting. Maybe everything that has happened has been a coincidence. Or someone outside stole information. There are thousands of hackers in this world who could have broken into the system and discovered any number of things."

"True. It's also possible someone working for the government or the military outside the bunker has the clearance to obtain information and make a buck on the side. Lord knows most of those people aren't paid enough."

"Exactly. So, when can we go back?" she pressed.

He groaned. "We don't even have permission to go back. I didn't single-handedly propose this arrangement, and I don't have the clout to undo it either. I'll talk to Temple and see if she can pull some strings on her end. It might help if she goes to bat for us with something more substantial than wanting to spend time with our son. Perhaps if she can show her superiors that we are a benefit to the team…"

Trish faced forward and sank farther into the cushions. She wasn't in the mood for bureaucratic red tape. She just wanted to go back to Colorado.

"I'll see what I can do," Tushar added.

They sat in silence for several seconds before Tushar's phone rang in his pocket. He released Trish's hand, lifted one hip to extract his cell, and took the call.

His face scrunched as he answered. "Davin?"

"There's been a perimeter breach."

Trish could hear every word. Her ear was only inches from Tushar's. She stiffened.

Tushar hesitated a moment. "Pardon?"

"The fence was cut along the south side of the ranch."

"What?" It seemed Tushar was struggling to catch up. He

shook his head, his free hand gripping Trish's thigh tighter than he probably realized. "When?"

"Just now. I have three men rushing to that location, but it's a distance away. You need to get out of there. Now."

Trish's heart raced, kicking up another notch as her adrenaline spiked.

Davin continued. "The fence is on an alarm. It went off two minutes ago. I can only tell which section. If someone knows you're here, they could also know about the cabin."

Tushar finally moved, jumping to his feet.

Trish followed, standing but then finding herself unable to move. She wasn't sure what to do. She watched Tushar rush around the cabin. He was still speaking to Davin, but she could no longer focus on the specifics. It was like the two of them were living in different planes. Tushar rushing around at high speed; Trish watching in slow motion.

When her husband thrust a coat at her, she somehow managed to grab it and shrug her arms into the sleeves as he pocketed the phone. His hand was on her cheek in an instant. "We need to leave. On foot. Quickly. Can you do it?"

She nodded. What if she had said no? She almost laughed. "You really think someone found us?"

"It would seem that way. Not taking any chances."

She glanced at the window. "What's the temperature?" At least it wasn't snowing. In fact, it hadn't snowed in a few days.

"It's cold." He rushed across the room to tug on boots and then a hat and scarf. Tucking thick gloves under his arm, he came back to her. "Trish?" His brow was furrowed. "We need to go."

She nodded, but couldn't manage to get her body to receive the flight message. Her brain was processing the urgency, but her arms and legs hadn't caught up to the adrenaline boost.

Tushar had her boots in his hand. He kneeled in front of her and lifted one foot to slide it into the thick lining. Moments later, he did the same with her other boot. He stood, zipped her coat up, tugged a hat over her head, and handed her a pair of mittens and a scarf.

"Trish?"

"I'm okay. I'm with you," she forced out, wrapping the warm scarf around her neck and then pulling on the mittens.

He didn't look convinced. He frowned, holding both her cheeks, his face inches away from hers. "We're going to be fine." Who was he kidding? Nothing about this arrangement was fine.

If they hadn't come to this remote cabin in Montana, they would be safe. She found it hard to believe the mob of protesters outside the bunker in Colorado had plans to force their way inside.

Running around a ranch in the dead of winter without much to protect them from the elements had to be the worst idea she'd ever heard.

Tushar turned around, found her phone on the kitchen counter, and tucked it into the pocket of her jeans. He grabbed her hand next, tugging her toward the cabin's only door. After yanking the door open, he picked up a backpack that had lain slumped on the floor for all these weeks.

Trish had never questioned its contents or asked why it was there. Now she realized it was probably filled with survival equipment. It was large and stuffed full.

"Let's go."

She followed, a cold blast of air hitting her face as soon as she stepped onto the porch. Damn, it was freezing. She pulled her hand free from Tushar to adjust her scarf to cover her cheeks. "Where are we going?"

"North." One word. Too vague.

"Tushar?"

He met her gaze again. "We have no choice." And then he jogged down the steps, reaching for her hand the second he hit the ground.

North? Just randomly north? With no destination in mind? "Are you sure this is necessary?"

"No. I'm not sure of anything. What I know is that someone cut the fence along the south side of the ranch. We have to assume it wasn't so they could steal a cow."

"Won't Davin and his people be able to handle it?"

"Yes. I'm certain they can. But we're not taking any chances. No one knows yet what we're facing. How many people. How armed they might be." Tushar was moving fast.

Trish had to jog to keep up with him. She wasn't in good enough shape for this. But she said nothing until they hit the tree line. Gasping for breath, she pulled her hand from his and stopped.

He wrapped an arm around her and hauled her against his chest. "Sorry about that. I wanted to get out of the clearing as fast as possible. We can slow down now." He tipped her head back with a gloved finger. "You okay?"

"I'm not sure. I can't do this, Tushar. I'm in no shape to run."

"I know." He kissed her forehead and released her. "Take a second. Catch your breath. Then we'll keep moving."

Deep breaths. Several of them. She was still heaving when he took her hand again. "I'm sorry. We need to move."

"Maybe it's nothing. Someone could have cut that fence for any number of reasons." God, she hoped that was the case.

"Maybe..." He didn't look at her.

She didn't argue further, mostly because she didn't have the breath to speak.

He picked their way between the trees, stepping carefully over branches and brush. "Try not to step on the snow," he encouraged.

She nodded, knowing he was worried about their tracks. Luckily the snow was in patches, easily avoidable. They continued like this for half an hour before Trish lifted her gaze to see them approaching the mountain range.

Tushar stopped walking and pulled her close again. Holding

her with one hand, he extracted his phone from his pocket with the other. "Good, we still have service." It rang in his hand before he could do anything else. "Give me good news, Davin. It's damn cold out here, and Trish isn't in shape for this."

Trish lifted onto her toes to listen.

"Sorry, man. Wish I could. We found the section of fence that was cut. It was definitely intentional. There's also an SUV parked a short distance away, marginally hidden off the side of the road. Whoever drove to that spot wasn't very smart if they didn't realize the fence is on my security system."

"Fuck."

"Yes. That sums it up."

"Any idea how many people we might be talking about?"

"Not yet. My men found at least two sets of prints, but they're nearly impossible to follow after they came through the fence. Where are you?"

"We moved north. Not fast. Maybe a mile from the cabin."

"Okay. If you can keep that up, you'll come to that stone ridge I told you about in another quarter mile. There are several indentations in the ridge that will provide at least the semblance of shelter on three sides."

Shelter?

"Got it. Thanks."

"You're going to lose cell service any minute now. I can't believe you still have any. I'm sending my men your direction. They should intersect you from the west."

"Okay. Thanks, Davin."

The called ended, and Trish met her husband's gaze. "We can't stay out here, Tushar." She was shaking her head in defiance and shock. "Not after dark."

"We might not have a choice." He reached back with one hand to tap the backpack. "I have provisions."

"Provisions?" Goose bumps rose all over her body. She shuddered. "You have a tent in there? Some sleeping bags?" She took a step back. Fear climbed up her spine to replace the adrenaline. The temperature was low. It would dip considerably lower when the sun went down.

"I have what we'll need. Let's keep moving."

She inhaled, trying to calm her nerves. Trying not to freak out or scream at him. "This is your plan? Keep moving? Hide in a small cave?"

"Yes." He frowned at her. "I didn't say it was ideal."

"But you planned this ahead of time. You had a backpack ready. You plotted it out with Davin."

He took a step closer. "Trish, I had backup plans. Yes."

"We should have taken the four-by-four. Why leave on foot?"

"We don't know what we're facing. We couldn't risk heading for the main entrance."

"You knew this might happen, and you kept it from me."

He blew out a breath. "I didn't know anything. I simply made plans for any eventuality."

Her voice rose. "And you didn't share them with me?"

He glanced around and then spoke barely above a whisper. "Let's not help out the enemy."

She replied through nearly gritted teeth. "You made this escape plan and didn't tell me. I'm hardly in good enough shape to walk across the room, and you thought it would be a great idea to trek through the woods toward the mountains at an altitude that's not conducive to breathing."

She had to give him credit for not walking away from her while she railed at him. But dammit.

He cleared his throat, stepped even closer, and whispered again. "Trish, you've hardly been speaking to me for three weeks. When was I supposed to share my escape plan? Would that have been while you were giving me the cold shoulder in bed with your back to me or while you were barricaded in the room avoiding me during the day?"

He was right. Of course. But she was still pissed. She jerked up her wrist and held it in front of his face. "And let's not forget we both have a GPS tracker in our damn arms. If that's what the enemy used to find us on this ranch, all we're doing is luring the bad guys away from civilization and trapping ourselves out in the middle of nowhere."

He nodded. He'd thought of that. She could tell by the look in his face. "We have to hope whatever intel someone might have came from a tip. It would be very difficult for someone to get into the system and use the GPS locator."

She nodded past him. "Fine. Let's go find these indentations you seem to think will resemble caves." She stepped past him, continuing toward the north.

CHAPTER 8

Tushar followed his wife the rest of the way to the base of the mountains, impressed by her ability to keep them headed in the right direction. Not that it would have been difficult. They were aiming for the damn mountains for heaven's sake.

She moved at a faster pace too, even though he knew it was too much for her. He felt bad. She hadn't left the cabin since they arrived three weeks ago. A month of PT could only do so much to help someone regain strength. She had no cardio under her belt at all. Not in over ten years, strictly speaking.

He tipped his head to one side several times, listening, constantly diligent. Aware of their surroundings. Praying he never heard any sound that was out of the ordinary. Where were Davin's men?

While they hiked, he silently slid a weapon from the pouch on the side of the backpack and palmed it. He had no interest in facing an unknown enemy alone, but if they were forced to confront someone, he wanted to be prepared. He hadn't taken it out while his wife was at his heels, but something was not right. The farther they moved, the more concerned he grew.

When she stopped suddenly, he ran into the back of her, steadying himself with his free hand to her waist.

Her gaze was focused on something up ahead, and he followed it to see a wolverine loping along in their line of sight. A full-grown adult animal. It didn't seem to notice them, or it didn't care, and after a few moments, it wandered out of sight.

Tushar pointed past the spot where the wolverine had stood. "Let's head for that indentation."

She kept walking and minutes later they were at the side of the mountain. "We'll be trapped here," she murmured.

"Hidden," he suggested. A rustling to his left made him spin around, gun raised, hoping to find the wolverine. Instead, he was relieved to see Jack making his way their direction.

"It's just me," Jack stated softly as he approached. He was smirking when he reached them, tugging his black facemask down to reveal his expression. "Not sure how I feel about those shooting refreshers we had in the last few weeks," he joked as he reached out, set a hand on Tushar's forearm, and gently lowered it toward the ground. "Your aim is probably greatly improved. I'd hate to get shot." Jack was dressed all in black from head to toe. He had a weapon in his hand and another strapped to his back.

Tushar rolled his eyes. "I've never shot anyone yet."

Jack lifted an eyelid. "Because you missed? Or because you've never tried?"

"Ha ha."

Trish sighed. "Whenever the two of you are done posturing, could we maybe hear the plan?"

Tushar reached out and grabbed her hand again to pull her in closer. If this threat had occurred yesterday or any time before that, he wouldn't have had the courage to so readily touch her as often as he had. But the truth was, they had made strides in the last twenty-four hours toward getting things right between them. He felt the need to keep her close, pull her into his side often, touch her. Even through the layers of mittens and coats and scarves.

Jack shifted his gaze to Trish. "Sorry. I'm also sorry to say I don't know much. Davin sent a man to the cabin to take off on the four-by-four. Hopefully if anyone was watching or listening, they will assume it was you. If not, they will at least presume you aren't at the cabin when they find it empty with no vehicle out front."

"Now what?" Trish asked.

"Now we wait." He pointed to a spot behind him and then another spot in a different direction. "I have two men with me. I'm going to join them, creating a perimeter. I'm sure you're exhausted. Why don't you sit down inside the cave and rest? It's not deep, but it will protect you from the wind. It's damn cold out here."

Trish turned around and made her way toward the small dark space.

"She okay?" Jack questioned.

"She will be." It was the only thing Tushar could think to say that wouldn't infuriate his wife further if she overheard. He left Jack without a word, to follow her.

She was facing the cave, standing just outside it, when he reached her side. "Cool plan. And by that I mean, freezing to death is exactly what I had in mind after spending ten years in a chilly state of vitrification." Her voice was so snarky, he had to bite his tongue to keep from making it worse.

"I have a Mylar blanket." He stepped around her, set his gun on the ground, and swung the backpack around to lower it also. After tugging out a bottle of water and the Mylar blanket, he motioned her over.

At least she closed the distance. He wasn't sure what he would do if she decided to keep up this angry defiance. Her safety was his number one priority, even though she didn't seem inclined to trust him on that front.

After shaking out the silver blanket, he lowered himself to the ground and reached for her. She didn't say anything, but she sat next to him, close enough for him to drape the wrap around both of them. He even risked circling her with his arm to pull her into his side.

After a few seconds, she leaned her cheek against his shoulder. "I'm sorry I'm being such a bitch. I hate this. I thought we were safe here. How the hell did someone find us?"

"I don't know, but trust me, it's the main thing on my mind. I keep running scenarios through my head, trying to figure out how it was possible. So few people know where we are."

"Do you suppose someone really could hack into the computers or phone or any other modern device and pull out the information?"

"It's possible, I guess. I'm not sure." A chill raced down his spine. The entire reason he had brought Trish to this remote cabin on a secure ranch in Montana was so she could recover in peace and find herself without the threat of being discovered or the constant daily barrage of people hassling them outside the bunker in Colorado.

He'd taken every precaution by permitting SURVIVE to sequester them. They'd come highly recommended. They were a strong force. He still trusted them even from this hiding spot against the mountain. Whoever might have found the two of them, Tushar would bet his life it had nothing to do with SURVIVE. The breech of information happened somewhere else.

Davin and his team were extremely well-respected. Their security was top-notch. No way in hell would they risk their livelihood by selling any of their clients short.

"I don't suppose it's possible whoever cut that fence was after something or someone else entirely," she murmured against his chest.

He squeezed her shoulder, not bothering to respond while he leaned his lips down to kiss the top of her head and inhale the scent of her shampoo. He couldn't remember if he'd ever smelled that particular mixture of strawberries and vanilla on her before.

Perhaps it hadn't even existed ten years ago. Someone could have simply provided her with it when she had her first shower six weeks ago. Honestly, he couldn't remember what she'd used before they were preserved. And that thought made him sad.

"Why didn't we take the four-by-four and head for the main house or get off this ranch?"

"Because that would be too obvious. Davin worried if anyone is after us, they're probably watching the house. They might not even know about the existence of the cabin."

She sighed.

He hated this for her. He hated it for himself too, but she didn't have as many weeks reanimated as he did. She was weak. Slower. Tired. Mentally and physically.

"We need to check in with Temple. ASAP. She needs to be aware of our situation," she stated.

She was right. In the mad dash to put distance between them and the possibly enemy, Tushar hadn't considered contacting Temple. He nodded against her head. "As soon as we can." If he could inform Temple or Ryan of their situation, one of them could at least track them and know their location.

She shuddered. "I've never been fond of knowing there's a GPS tracker in my arm. It might come in handy today, but it's disconcerting knowing anyone can find us at any time."

"Yeah. When Ryan first told me, I cringed. It felt invasive. But since it was Ryan, I trust his reasoning for agreeing to the tracking devices in all of us. Besides, he explained that with today's technology, it hardly matters. Our phones can be tracked just as easily. Since we each have one in our pocket, the GPS device hardly matters."

"I'm not sure that makes me feel warm and fuzzy either. So many changes in a decade." Her voice trailed off.

He held her in silence for a few minutes.

"I'd also like an update on the protesters. Maybe they've dwindled in our absence, making it easier for us to sneak back inside without anyone becoming aware."

"It's possible."

She lifted her gaze to face him. "I'm not willing to live like this. On the run. Always worried. We don't even know if this particular scare is legitimate, and yet here we are, in the cold, resting in a cave against a mountain." She shook her head vehemently. "I won't do this again, Tushar. Once is enough. When we get out of this mess, I want to go home."

He knew what she meant by *home*. Not just the house they had lived in before being preserved, but the bunker itself where they'd spent the majority of their time. The house was still there. Trish's mother had been living in it all this time. But the bunker was what she thought of as home.

Tushar could no longer deny his wife's request. She was right. If they were going to be pursued all over the country anyway, they would be safer inside the bunker. "Okay. I'll talk Temple into it. We'll make it happen." He would do this. For her. Even if he had to defy orders.

"What about Dade? Has anyone found about Dade's existence yet?"

"No. Thank God." Dade was the fourth member of the team to be revived. In the two weeks since he'd been revived, not a word of his existence had been breathed. The secrecy of his reanimation was easier because he didn't have any close relatives who needed to be informed.

In the past several months, the bunker had acquired the funding to get additional reanimation chambers. Now four more people were currently being reanimated at the same time— another fact under wraps from the public. So far.

"Doesn't that raise a red flag in and of itself? I mean, if Dade's existence hasn't been leaked, there is little chance a mole is operating from inside the bunker."

"You have a point." He stopped stroking her hair to consider her words. "I'm not sure I like that idea better or worse. The thought that someone higher up in the government or the military is sharing classified information with the outside world is almost less palatable than thinking it's one of our own."

She shuddered under his touch. "You're right. There's also no chance the next people to be revived can be kept secret. Now that there are three additional chambers, four new people will come out of their preservation in a few weeks. They have families and friends waiting for them. They've already started calling to find out when their loved ones might also be revived. Nothing about our existence can be kept under wraps for much longer."

The truth was that the entire project was about to draw international attention. It had been trial and error handling the first reanimation—Emily—as people she had known ten years ago learned of her preservation. With Tushar and Trish, they had each other and her mother to consider. Tushar had been in contact with his own parents also, but they would never breathe a word to anyone alive.

Dade was an easy case too since he didn't have many connections outside the bunker. But things were about to get dicey. Times four. And then fourteen more souls.

Tushar knew Temple and several others were working frantically on plans to keep things from getting out of control with public perception, but it would not be an easy road.

Tushar could help. So could Trish.

As if Trish were thinking along the same lines as him again, she said, "Things are going to get complicated."

"Yes."

"I can't stand the thought that there's a mole on Ryan's team. It would kill him to find out someone he's been working with for the last few years was selling information to the very people who kidnapped Emily."

"I've thought of that. I'm sure it's stressful for him, but he hasn't mentioned anything to me." Though Tushar was certain from the furrow he'd often seen on his son's brow that Ryan was worried. "Let's hope it's no one we know. Temple has superiors we've never met. Plus, there is the team of active military and security guards protecting the bunker. Could even be someone Emily came in contact with. There's no way to ever find out, most likely. But I sure would like the threats to stop."

His hope was that whoever was selling their information got bored or tapped out. With an increasing number of reanimations, perhaps the saturation of information would get less interesting to the public at large.

Leaking the existence of the revived wasn't meant to be a secret forever, but Tushar shuddered every time he considered the amount of information someone seemed to have collected.

They sat in silence for a few minutes, Trish shivering slightly in his embrace. He pulled her tighter. "I'm sorry."

"I know." She sighed against him. "Me too."

He lifted his free hand and tipped her chin back to meet her gaze.

Her eyes were wide and trusting, the anger having dissipated.

When he lowered his lips to hers, she let him. The kiss was brief and soft. The heat of the last twenty-four hours flooded his mind. He wanted that back. Why did this shit have to happen to stop the perfect reconciliation and make his wife angry all over again?

"I hate that you were suffocating in the bunker," she stated as their lips parted. "I didn't know. I was only thinking of myself. I wanted more time with Ryan. It wasn't enough." She wiped a tear from her cheek that brought a knot to his throat. She had been hurting for three weeks, and he had done nothing to help her. Instead, he'd stubbornly left her to absorb all that pain alone.

"I know. I should have explained things better. I made a mistake. It won't happen again. I thought I was protecting you." *Instead, I made things worse.*

She nodded, taking a deep breath and closing her eyes as if to swallow back the tears.

"We'll go back. I promise. As soon as it's reasonably safe."

Another slow nod. "Thank you."

He shrugged. "I know I need to be there leading the team as they each come out of preservation. We both do. I just felt so... helpless. Out of my element. I don't know the latest medical advances. It was very frustrating. I didn't even know anything about the process of reanimation. It was torture waiting for you to be revived while I scrambled to understand the reanimation chamber and how it works."

She grabbed his hand and held it to her chest. "I'm sure I would have been just as frustrated as you if it had been me to wake up first."

He set his forehead against hers, closing his eyes to absorb her comforting words two seconds before a shot rang out.

CHAPTER 9

Trish jumped to her feet so fast she lost her balance.

Luckily, Tushar grabbed her arm, pulled her farther into the darkness of the cave, and stepped in front of her. His gun was in his hand. Raised. Alert. Ready.

"Shit," she whispered. "You have another weapon? I can't just hide behind you." *What the hell was I thinking?* This was serious. She shouldn't have been so apathetic about this situation. She'd either been in denial about the level of danger or simply defiant. Both could get her killed if she didn't snap out of it and pay attention.

Tushar kneeled down quickly, lifted the opening of the backpack, and snagged another weapon. He set it in her palm. "You remember how to shoot this thing?"

She assumed he was joking and rolled her eyes. For all intents and purposes she had last participated in shooting practice months ago by her mental calendar, during a training session. After all, she had been a lieutenant in the army, same as Tushar, before they had gotten sick.

Palming the Glock, she took a deep breath and forced her

mind to calm. They wouldn't survive this if she didn't get a grip on her emotions.

Another shot rang out and someone shouted.

"Fuck," Tushar muttered under his breath. "We're sitting ducks here. Can't tell if the shots are friendly or hostile." He grabbed her hand. "Can you run?"

"Yes." She could do anything now that her adrenaline was pumping.

He met her gaze, lowering his voice further. "Stay right on my flank. I'm going to skirt the edge of this mountain, heading north."

She nodded.

He hastily zipped up the backpack and shrugged it onto his shoulders. "Let's go." And then he was on the move.

She stayed right behind him, her gaze scanning constantly. Silence. Not a single person in her line of sight. The absence of Jack or either of his men made her skin crawl with unease.

And they had another problem. How the hell were they going to identify anyone they saw as friendly or not? The enemy could easily be dressed in the same dark clothing as the men protecting them.

As they slinked as silently as possible away from the small cave, Trish held her breath for long seconds at a time, trying to ensure she could hear every twig or branch or rustling in the brush. The crunch of snow. The swish of warm clothing as it rubbed against itself. Anything.

They moved along slowly, carefully picking their way forward while avoiding making any more noise than necessary.

Tushar glanced back at her several times, but he didn't coddle her. They were both equally trained for combat situations—which meant very little since neither of them had ever seen combat. She needed her husband to pay attention to the possible enemy, however, not her.

Adrenaline pumping, she kept up with him easily. She might have initially doubted the intentions of whoever had cut the fence and made their way onto the ranch property, but there was little doubt now of their intent. Gunfire cleared that up.

SURVIVE was the best in the world at what they did, however. She felt confident they were actively in pursuit.

Another shot made her hesitate, and she had to bite her lip to keep from making any noise as three more shots rang out. She hated the thought that any of the men who worked for Davin might lose their lives protecting her and Tushar.

When Tushar came to a halt in front of her, Trish glanced at him and then followed his line of sight. He was nodding.

Thank God. One of Davin's men was yards away, making hand signals to indicate which direction they should head. As Trish and her husband made their way behind the completely black-clad member of SURVIVE, he scanned the area, gun held up and ready. He glanced at Trish and nodded as she passed by.

Another series of hand signals indicated the best path, and five minutes later Trish eased into another cave along the base of the mountain, this one larger than the last.

She held her breath intermittently, listening intently. For several minutes she heard nothing but the sounds of nature. Their protector was no longer in sight, and she imagined him setting up a perimeter. Surely Davin's men had a means of communication between them.

Tushar wrapped his hand around her forearm and handed her a water bottle. She took a sip and gave it back. While he was reaching behind himself to tuck the bottle back in his pack, another hand grabbed Trish's arm, this one with much more force.

She twisted her head to find the man who'd led them to safety staring down at her. For a moment, relief flooded her body, and then she noted the look in his eyes. This was not one of Davin's men. This was the enemy.

"What the hell are you doing?" Tushar growled.

The man yanked Trish in front of him, knocked her weapon

out of her hand, and put his gun to her temple. "Drop your gun or she's dead."

Oh my God. Oh my God. Trish's body stiffened as she found herself pressed against this guy's chest. Her scarf fell away from her face, and her hat fell off her head to land on the ground. She couldn't breathe. Fear slammed into her, making it difficult to think. Her gaze followed Tushar as he set his gun on the ground and then lifted his hands in the air. "There's no reason for anyone to get hurt. Tell me what you want, and I'll make it happen."

The guy growled. His next words were low and deep and barely above a whisper. "What I want right now is for you to shut the fuck up. Not a sound. If either of you makes a sound, I will shoot you both without flinching. I don't care if I take you alive or leave you here dead."

That last part unnerved Trish on a new level. What was the aim of these people if they didn't want her or Tushar alive? She couldn't wrap her head around that reality. The situation was far more dire than she expected if whoever hired this guy had given him permission to kidnap *or* kill.

The look on Tushar's face and the widening of his eyes told Trish he was thinking the same thing. He tugged his scarf down so she could see his entire expression.

Trish flinched against her captor's chest when more shots sounded in the vicinity. How many men were with him? Did Davin's men know one of the bad guys was holding her and Tushar hostage?

The guy was huge. Over six feet and he outweighed her by over a hundred pounds. The grip he had on her arm as he held her against his frame was firm enough to break the bone if he wanted.

The cold metal at her temple was a constant reminder that he had no problem shooting her in the head and leaving her there to die.

She scrambled to keep her feet under her as he dragged her toward the edge of the cave. Cold air hit her face, stinging her eyes as her cheeks flushed hot. "Stay where I can see you." He removed the barrel from her forehead to point to a spot across from him where he intended Tushar to stand. And then he scanned the area. What was he hoping for? A signal? Help?

His accent indicated he was from somewhere in the south, but his features were completely covered with a black mask that permitted her no details to describe him.

Tushar was staring at her, and she held his gaze, hoping whatever he intended to communicate would somehow travel between them. He was scowling, however, and his stance was stiff. He also paid no attention to the outside of the cave. His entire focus was on her with small glances to the movements of her captor.

God, she wished she could read his mind. She did not get the impression he was simply taking her in. He had a plan. An idea.

Another round of shots. Too many to count. Someone had a semi-automatic weapon. She prayed it was one of the good guys.

Shouts indicated people were close by. That was a good sign, but it sounded like a war zone, or at least what she would expect a war zone to sound like. For a moment she regretted having never been in a combat situation. Maybe she would be better equipped to handle this scenario if she had been.

She was shocked by her ability to hold the fear at bay and concentrate on how they were going to get out of this. She was alert and aware of every sound. Every voice. Every shot. The crunch of boots. Voices. Instead of a full-fledged panic, she went into fight mode. She certainly had no intention of dying on this mountain when she had so much left to do in this life.

The man holding her never released his grip on her wrist, nor did he lower his gun from her head as he seemed to be waiting for instructions or communication from someone.

Every glance at Tushar solidified her thought that he was formulating a plan. He was also inching closer.

She couldn't imagine what he intended to do since he was

significantly shorter and less bulky than the man holding her. It wasn't as though he could knock the gun from the guy's hand or jump him. On the flip side, the determination on his face reminded her Tushar indeed had a more vested interest in keeping her alive than the two fucks her captor gave about whether or not she died.

While the bulky brute leaned out of the cave to get a better view, Tushar's gaze darted around, his eyes wide.

Trish knew he was trying to communicate with her. She watched him intently, somehow managing to ignore the cold wind as it struck her in the face. Her hair was damp from wearing the hat, and now she was losing heat from her scalp.

Tushar's gaze narrowed on her. She held it and watched as he glanced down and then back up. Again. And again. Rapid flickering of his eyes toward the ground. If he wanted her to go limp and drop to the ground, he was crazy. She wasn't holding herself up with any effort at all. The man was holding her like a rag doll.

She narrowed her gaze, hoping to convey the impossibility of his suggestion—if that's what it was.

Shots grew closer. Shouting was louder. And then a second man stepped into view. She realized he was on the wrong team when he nodded at her captor and glanced at Tushar.

"Grab the scientist. Let's go," the man holding her ordered.

Dammit. This was not good.

But just as the newcomer reached out toward Tushar, another shot rang out. It must have hit the guy in the back of the head. His eyes widened for a second, and then he dropped face-first to the ground.

"Fuck," the man holding Trish shouted.

"Now," Tushar yelled a moment later.

Trish realized her captor had relaxed his hold on her the moment his partner hit the ground. She gave a quick jerk in his grip and managed to slide down his body several inches, causing him to lose his hold on her. He had to lower his gun in an attempt to keep from losing her.

The last thing Trish thought before a second shot rang out was how the hell this maneuver was going to be helpful. And then her ears were ringing and she was falling, being pulled toward the ground by the heavy weight of the man at her back.

She jerked her gaze to Tushar to find him lowering a gun as he rushed forward. Warm liquid slid across her cheek as her captor slumped all the way forward, pinning her to the ground. She scrambled to get out from under the dead weight, shoving at his chest until Tushar managed to lift him off her and grab her arm.

Her heart was racing as she scampered away from the man and turned to look back. Tushar had shot him in the forehead. His eyes were still open. His lips parted.

She closed her eyes as her husband pulled her into his embrace and then wiped the blood from her face with the corner of his scarf. His eyes were narrowed. "You okay?"

All she could do was nod before shadows forced them to spin around and face the entrance to the cave. Davin's frame blocked the light, two men flanking him. He was breathing heavily as he took in the scene.

She didn't need anyone to tell her it was over. She simply closed her eyes and leaned against Tushar, dipping her face into his chest while she tried to catch her breath. "I want this goddamn tracker removed from my arm ASAP."

"Agreed." He held her tighter.

CHAPTER 10

Two days later…

Trish blinked her eyes open as a crick in her neck made her wince. It only took a second to remember where she was.

She lifted a hand to rub out the kinks on her shoulder and stared out the windshield before glancing at Tushar. "How long was I asleep?"

"A few hours." He was smiling when he glanced at her before returning his focus to the road.

"You want me to drive for a while?"

"No. I'm stopping at the next exit for the night anyway. We're about halfway home. We should arrive by afternoon tomorrow. It's only about six more hours." He reached for her hand and brought it to his lap. His thumb brushing over the back of her hand was soothing.

Home. She liked the sound of that. There was no way to predict what the future might look like, but as long as they were back in Colorado, close enough to see Ryan and Emily on a regular basis, she would be able to breathe easily.

They faced a long road of uncertainty, but she felt stronger now than a month ago. She knew she could be of help in the bunker as the rest of the team came back to the living. There was a lot to be done and so many unanswered questions.

Tushar was much more relaxed about their return than he had been two days ago. He seemed eager instead of reluctant. She wasn't sure if his change of heart was due to their near-death experience, or if he was finally ready to sink his mind back into research. In either case, it had been interesting listening to him reason with Temple on the phone as he convinced her they would be safer inside the bunker where they could also be of use to the new research team in some capacity.

The two men who had tried to capture them were both dead. That made it very difficult to find out who hired them and why. It was unnerving, and although Tushar had spoken to Temple at length about the possibilities, both of them had done nothing more than bang their heads against the wall.

Was it a coincidence that someone had also abducted Emily? Were the two incidents in any way related? It seemed impossible. The man who had taken Emily was a distraught father of a preserved child who died of leukemia. He was in jail awaiting trial. It was ludicrous to think he would have orchestrated something else from behind bars. And why would he?

In the end, it seemed there could be no connection. Random groups of people had separate agendas when it came to the team of reanimated people. Every member of the team would need to be diligent for their entire lives.

Trish's conversations with Temple had largely centered around the idea of giving everyone who was willing new identities. Emily had toyed with the idea herself, but falling in love with Ryan had put a period on that idea. Trish and Tushar had zero interest in reinventing themselves and leaving Ryan, so it was out of the question. The concept would be posed to Dade and then the rest of the team, however.

She couldn't imagine how many of them would take Temple up on the idea. No matter how long they had been preserved, every member of the team would wake up a scientist just as they'd been when they entered the cryostats. Who among them would give up their life's work in order to preserve their safety?

This was a questions each team member would have to answer for themselves. But Trish intended to be there for everyone from now on. She was strong. She could do anything, and one day she would be refreshed enough in medicine to reenter the lab. Tushar would too.

Trish plopped down on the bed as soon as they entered the hotel room and stared at the ceiling. "I shouldn't be tired. I slept most of the way here."

Tushar perched on the edge of the mattress and rested a hand on her thigh. "You've been through a lot. More than most humans endure in a lifetime."

She tipped her head his direction. "What do you mean? All I did was take a three-week vacation on a gorgeous Montana ranch," she joked, a giggle escaping her lips as she rolled toward him and propped her head up on one hand.

He shrugged. "Right. I mean who would count the ten-year hibernation, weeks of physical therapy, finding out your kid is thirty, oh, and narrowly escaping death by two madmen?"

She laughed again. "Semantics."

He smiled at her, his face sobering as he smoothed his hand up her body and then cupped her face. "I like that sound."

"What sound?" She tried to imagine what he was referring to in the silent room.

"Your laughter. I haven't heard it in a long time."

She tipped her face into his palm and planted a kiss on the smooth skin. "I was napping. It was hard to laugh."

"Napping? Is that what we're calling it now? Shall we tell the other team members they were taking a nap as they wake up?"

She smiled. "It's not a bad idea."

He released her face and gave her a shove so that she fell onto her back. Two seconds later he was on the bed, straddling her body, his hands holding him aloft on both sides of her head. "Do it again."

"What?" she asked, batting her eyes. This new Tushar was intriguing. He'd shown her a side of himself she couldn't remember just days ago, and here he was doing it again. Sexy. Playful. Dominant.

He sat up, grabbed her hands, and hauled them over her head. After securing both wrists in one hand, he lowered the other one to her side and trailed one finger up from her hip to her armpit.

She squirmed, laughing again. "Hey…"

"That's it. I really, really like that sound. From now on I want to hear it every day or you're going to find yourself pinned down while I tickle you."

She smiled broadly at the excitement in his expression, but a flush crept up her face at the same time. "Mmm."

"What?" He lifted a brow.

"I'm not sure which path I'll choose."

He smirked. "You like being tickled?"

She shook her head. "No. But I think I like being pinned down." The flush spread, heating her face.

One second she was biting her lip, shocked by her innuendo. The next second Tushar's mouth was on hers, his lips hard and demanding. She parted for him, loving the feel of his kiss and the way her entire body responded to his touch. When she gave a tug on her hands and came up short, unable to break free, a moan escaped her mouth.

Oh. My. God. Where had this side of Tushar been hiding all these years? She wiggled, conscious of the wetness in her panties and the way her nipples pressed against her bra.

When his hand flattened on her belly and smoothed up to cup her breast, she arched into his chest. He didn't break the kiss as he molded his fingers to her sensitive skin and then pinched her nipple through the layers.

Finally, just when she thought she might combust, he parted from her mouth and rose above her. His hands went to the hem of her sweater to tug it over her head. His gaze never left hers except for the second the material blocked their view.

His chest rose and fell with every deep breath. "I love the sound of your laughter, but I'm even more interested in the way you moan when you're aroused."

More heat infused her cheeks. Why was she so easily embarrassed with her own husband of over twenty years?

She knew the answer to that question. It had been a long time since they really took the time to enjoy one another. They'd had sex from time to time when it seemed obligatory because weeks had gone by, but she couldn't remember if there was ever a time when they played like this.

She watched her husband intently as he removed the rest of her clothes and then his own. Soon he was hovering over her again, his erection bobbing against her belly. He threaded their fingers together and planted their hands at the sides of her head. "You're sexier than the day we met."

She smiled. "You are too. I'm sorry we didn't nurture this side of us. Let's make a vow to never let that happen again."

He nodded. "Promise."

"I love you."

"I love you, too."

"Now stop teasing me and get to work nurturing this newly found sex drive. I like it."

He slid between her legs, holding her gaze. As he thrust into her, she gasped. It felt so good. Right. Perfect. Home.

"Mmm, maybe I like that gasp you make even more. Do it again." He pulled out a few inches and thrust back in.

She gave him what he wanted, but only because there was no way to stop herself.

AUTHOR'S NOTE

I hope you enjoyed this second book in the *Project DEEP* series. Please enjoy the following excerpt for book three in the series, *Reviving Dade*.

REVIVING DADE

PROJECT DEEP (BOOK THREE)

"The Notebook? Are you serious?" Blair stared at Emily hard, forcing herself not to roll her eyes. Chick flicks were not her thing, especially not sappy ones. But Emily was the one who'd missed out on over ten years' worth of movies, so Blair wasn't about to say a word. If her friend wanted to spend the evening crying over Nicholas Sparks, Blair would endure it.

Emily giggled as she opened the fridge. "Hey, I read the book, but I never got to see the movie."

"I'm pretty sure it's older than ten years," Blair pointed out, as she took a beer from Emily's hand and shoved her hip off the counter.

"Do you think I had a lot of free time in the few years before I was preserved?" Emily asked.

She had a point. Before she'd been cryonically preserved for the past ten years, she had spent several years buried in this bunker working for the government on Project DEEP (Disease & Epidemic Eradication & Prevention). The final disease she had been studying, frantically working toward a cure, had also been the one to land her, twenty other team members, and General Winston Custodio in cryostats. Thanks to a freak lab accident,

AP12, a fatal viral form of anemia, infected everyone in the medical wing.

"Considering the work ethic you've demonstrated since I met you, I'm going to say probably not," Blair replied. Emily worked night and day.

So did her boyfriend, Ryan Anand, who was currently sitting at the kitchen table on the other side of the room with his head buried in his computer and his brow furrowed. Both of them were as dedicated to their work as any human Blair had ever met.

In fact, it must be an affliction all these medical researchers suffered from because both of Ryan's parents had been reanimated in the last few months too, and they were equally dedicated workhorses.

Emily held a soda in her hand as she plopped down on the couch. "I'm not sure you're actually allowed to drink beer while you watch Nicholas Sparks, but I'll let it slide," she joked.

"I'm not sure you're allowed to watch anything while sitting this close to the television," she returned, also teasing. Ryan and Emily lived inside the bunker in one of the new suites that were built a few years ago to house the full-time employees. The living room area was incredibly tight.

"Fuck," Ryan suddenly shouted. He followed that by launching his pen at the wall and then shoving his chair back. Hand threaded in his hair, he turned toward them. His face was red.

Emily jumped up from the couch, set her soda on the coffee table, and faced Ryan. "What happened?"

Blair's teeth were on edge. She'd known Ryan for a very long time, and she'd never seen him lose his cool. Not once. Something he was working on had apparently seriously pissed him off.

His chest rose and fell with every breath.

"Ryan?" Emily said, her voice lower. She had known Ryan for six months, ever since she had been the first person to be reanimated from the original Project DEEP team.

He released his hair to run a hand down his face. "We have a problem."

"What is it?" Emily asked.

Blair felt out of place, as if she shouldn't be here. But it couldn't be helped. She would feel even more awkward about easing out of the suite.

"We can't give Dade the cure." His shoulders fell as he spoke.

Dade Menke was scheduled to come out of his coma the next day. After four weeks in the reanimation chamber, each patient then spent four weeks in an induced coma to allow their organs to fully rejuvenate before they were awakened.

Blair knew a great deal of the details. Assigned to security detail at this bunker for the last seven years, she was as informed as possible about what the team of medical researchers did at the facility.

Emily eased across the room and set a hand on Ryan's arm. "Why not?"

"He's got the genetic marker for aplastic anemia 2. I can't believe I didn't see this in his charts before now."

"Oh, no. Ryan, I'm so sorry."

Blair couldn't keep herself from asking questions. She had no idea what they were talking about, but it had to be bad. "What does that mean?"

Emily turned around. "Aplastic anemia is when the bone marrow stops producing enough blood cells. Unfortunately there have been several instances in the last year when patients were given the treatment for AP12 only to have it jumpstart latent aplastic anemia they didn't even know they carried. AA2 is a mutation of the common form."

"So you can't give him the cure for AP12 because it will kill him?"

"Basically," Ryan stated. "Dammit. The guy is thirty-five years old. He's just spent ten years suspended in time. I can't believe when he wakes up tomorrow, I have to tell him he's still going to die."

Emily wiped her eyes as she headed across the room to grab a tissue. She would be the one in the room to take this the hardest. Dade had been her coworker. Blair hadn't been there ten years ago. And Ryan, who had dedicated his entire life to finding a cure and putting together a new team to reanimate the first team, was only twenty when everyone was preserved.

"Project DEEP has been working on a cure for AA2 for months now. Maybe..." Emily's voice wavered.

Blair could only surmise that most likely Emily was grasping at straws. Blair knew next to nothing about medical research, but she was smart enough to realize it took years to find a cure for any disease. Dade wouldn't have that kind of time.

Even though she had never met the guy and she hadn't even seen pictures of him, her heart seized to hear his age. She too was thirty-five. She couldn't imagine someone coming to her tomorrow to tell her they had the cure for her first fatal disease but injecting it would give her another equally fatal disease.

Emily's voice was soft when she asked her next question. "How much time do you think he might have if you don't give him the AP12 cure and instead work against the symptoms?"

"I don't know. We've proven that the total blood replacement he received a month ago will buy him time. It worked for you. But in your case, we only waited three weeks. There's no way to know when you would have developed AP12 symptoms. And when we reanimated my parents, we gave them the treatment immediately." He pulled his chair back to the table and pushed it in.

Blair hated seeing him this defeated. Emily too. What a blow to their research.

Ryan closed his computer and picked it up. "I'm going to go work in the lab. You two enjoy your movie." He kissed Emily on the cheek and left the suite.

There was no way in the world they could sit and watch a sad movie after that revelation, but Blair took her seat anyway. Emily would need a friend.

The two of them had met only five months ago when Blair was assigned to Emily's protection for one day, but they had bonded and formed a friendship that would last a lifetime.

After a few minutes of silence, Emily sat up straighter. "The media will have a field day with this. Shit. Plus, the rest of the reanimations could be compromised if he dies. The government might force us to slow down to be certain every member will survive." She slapped her forehead with her palm.

Blair cringed. "Can we keep the media from finding out, at least?"

Emily chuckled wryly. "Sure. Like we kept them from finding out about me and then Tushar and Trish. How long did that last? All of twenty-four hours? The vultures are just waiting for a mistake."

ALSO BY BECCA JAMESON

Seattle Doms:

Salacious Exposure by Becca Jameson

Salacious Desires By Kate Oliver

Salacious Attraction by Becca Jameson

Salacious Indulgence by Kate Oliver

Salacious Devotion by Becca Jameson

Salacious Surrender by Kate Oliver

Danger Bluff:

Rocco

Hawking

Kestrel

Magnus

Phoenix

Caesar

Roses and Thorns:

Marigold

Oleander

Jasmine

Tulip

Daffodil

Lily

Roses and Thorns Box Set One

Roses and Thorns Box Set Two

Nonstop

Standby

Takeoff

Jetway

Open Skies Box Set One

Open Skies Box Set Two

Shadow SEALs:

Shadow in the Desert

Shadow in the Darkness

Holt Agency:

Rescued by Becca Jameson

Unchained by KaLyn Cooper

Protected by Becca Jameson

Liberated by KaLyn Cooper

Defended by Becca Jameson

Unrestrained by KaLyn Cooper

Delta Team Three (Special Forces: Operation Alpha):

Destiny's Delta

Canyon Springs:

Caleb's Mate

Hunter's Mate

Corked and Tapped:

Volume One: Friday Night

Volume Two: Company Party

Volume Three: The Holidays

The Complete Set

Tempting Elizabeth

Club Zodiac Box Set One

Club Zodiac Box Set Two

Club Zodiac Box Set Three

The Art of Kink:

Pose

Paint

Sculpt

Arcadian Bears:

Grizzly Mountain

Grizzly Beginning

Grizzly Secret

Grizzly Promise

Grizzly Survival

Grizzly Perfection

Arcadian Bears Box Set One

Arcadian Bears Box Set Two

Sleeper SEALs:

Saving Zola

Spring Training:

Catching Zia

Catching Lily

Catching Ava

Spring Training Box Set

The Underground series:

Force

Clinch

Guard

Submit

Thrust

Torque

The Underground Box Set One

The Underground Box Set Two

Wolf Masters series:

Kara's Wolves

Lindsey's Wolves

Jessica's Wolves

Alyssa's Wolves

Tessa's Wolf

Rebecca's Wolves

Melinda's Wolves

Laurie's Wolves

Amanda's Wolves

Sharon's Wolves

Wolf Masters Box Set One

Wolf Masters Box Set Two

Claiming Her series:

The Rules

The Game

The Prize

Claiming Her Box Set

Emergence series:

Bound to be Taken

Bound to be Tamed

Bound to be Tested

Bound to be Tempted

Emergence Box Set

The Fight Club series:

Come

Perv

Need

Hers

Want

Lust

The Fight Club Box Set One

The Fight Club Box Set Two

Wolf Gatherings series:

Tarnished

Dominated

Completed

Redeemed

Abandoned

Betrayed

Wolf Gatherings Box Set One

Wolf Gathering Box Set Two

Durham Wolves series:

Rescue in the Smokies

Fire in the Smokies

Freedom in the Smokies

Durham Wolves Box Set

Stand Alone Books:

Blind with Love

Guarding the Truth

Out of the Smoke

Abducting His Mate

Wolf Trinity

Frostbitten

A Princess for Cale/A Princess for Cain

Severed Dreams

Where Alphas Dominate

ABOUT THE AUTHOR

Becca Jameson is a USA Today best-selling author of over 150 books. She is well-known for her Wolf Masters series, her Fight Club series, and her Surrender series. She currently lives in Houston, Texas, with her husband. Two grown kids pop in every once in a while, too! She is loving this journey and has dabbled in a variety of genres, including paranormal, sports romance, military, reverse harem, dark romance, suspense, dystopian, BDSM, and Daddy Dom.

A total night owl, Becca writes late at night, sequestering herself in her office with a glass of red wine and a bar of dark chocolate, her fingers flying across the keyboard as her characters weave their own stories.

During the day--which never starts before ten in the morning!-- she can be found walking, running errands, or reading in her favorite hammock chair!

...where Alphas dominate...

Becca's Newsletter Sign-up

Join my Facebook fan group, Becca's Bibliomaniacs, for the most up-to-date information, random excerpts while I work, giveaways, and fun release parties!

Facebook Fan Group:
Becca's Bibliomaniacs

Contact Becca:
www.beccajameson.com
beccajameson4@aol.com

facebook.com/becca.jameson.18
x.com/beccajameson
instagram.com/becca.jameson
bookbub.com/authors/becca-jameson
goodreads.com/beccajameson
amazon.com/author/beccajameson

www.ingramcontent.com/pod-product-compliance
Lightning Source LLC
Chambersburg PA
CBHW051308170626
46809CB00004B/1794

* 9 7 8 1 9 4 6 9 1 1 4 5 2 *